UNPACKING YESTERDAY

July 2020

UNPACKING YESTERDAY

BROTHERHOOD'S LEGACY

Elizabeth Rieman

Steadfast & Loyal!
Beth Rieman

Deeds Publishing | Athens

Copyright © 2020—Elizabeth Rieman

ALL RIGHTS RESERVED—No part of this book may be reproduced in any form or by any electronic or mechanical means, including information storage and retrieval systems, without permission in writing from the authors, except by a reviewer who may quote brief passages in a review.

Published by Deeds Publishing in Athens, GA
www.deedspublishing.com

Printed in The United States of America

Cover design by Mark Babcock.

ISBN 978-1-950794-22-5

Books are available in quantity for promotional or premium use. For information, email info@deedspublishing.com.

First Edition, 2020

10 9 8 7 6 5 4 3 2 1

To Vincent.

May the decisions you make, in reaction to events beyond your control, continue to be shaped by the examples of your many courageous ancestors. May the legacy you leave behind be just as inspiring.

CONTENTS

To the Reader	xi
Prologue	xiii
Correspondence	1–264
Author's Note	265
Additional Facts	269
Acknowledgements	287
About the Author	291

TO THE READER

This story is a unique combination of both fact and fiction, with well researched scenes depicting specific battles in the European theater of WWII and authentic characters who are real people, embellished by my imagination. Though at times I was able to include some of the actual words and phrases used, the journal entries and letters in this book are of my imagination, presented as if Teddy's and Uncle Jim's writings were preserved in time. Though I made every attempt to match tone and personality for each person, their voices are my own. Anchoring this narrative is an unembellished history of the 4th Infantry Division's involvement in WWII, specifically from January 1944 until the end of the war in Europe—VE Day on 8 May 1945. After personally researching, consulting with military experts, and interviewing historians, I have attempted to present the 4th Infantry Division's actions accurately and I have not consciously altered any facts.

As a presenter, I speak regularly to groups of veterans and diverse audiences, sharing this story, my research related to WWII, and my visit to France where I donated a precious piece of my family's history to the Utah Beach Museum. As a teacher, I have shared the story and the connected artifacts with groups of students who have been inspired by "The Greatest Generation." As a reader of WWII historical fiction, I have not come across many recent WWII novels, outside the nonfiction realm, that center primarily on the soldier's experience and the deep friendships that are forged in times of war. It is my hope that this story will open that world to you, the reader, as you are taken down your own path of discovery, learning about two great men, a war that changed the world, and legacy's lasting impact.

—Elizabeth Rieman

PROLOGUE

I have often heard it said that each step we take in life is a choice, and the sum of those choices is what life becomes. I know, in my life, this is mostly true. However, I don't think we can discount the events over which we have absolutely no control, the events which, when compiled, shape our lives as well. Tragedy, loss, or even "fate" cannot be removed from the equation. Looking back over the past year, I now believe that life is made up of events beyond our capacity to control or to even understand in their immediacy, and that it is our *reactions* to these events, our choices in *how we respond*, that make our lives what they are. Our everyday choices certainly impact our realities, but so often, it is the choices we are forced to make, in reaction to the obstacles thrown in our paths, that truly define us.

When I went home that summer to spend time alone with my parents, I wanted to sift through my Grandma Rose's boxes—boxes she had left behind so many years ago, sealed and unopened. I knew the boxes were full of family stories that I had an urgency to know—stories of people I had never met but with whom I wanted to connect, lost legacies I wanted to learn.

My grandmother's ancestral line was particularly interesting to me, and her childhood had a specifically morbid appeal to me. The stories she told were sad, but they were less emotionally impactful to me than they were alluring because I had not yet truly immersed myself in them; I had not come close to empathizing with the people involved.

Yet.

Grandma Rose's father (my great-grandfather), Robert, died in 1924, when she was just 18 months old. He was riding his bicycle home from work and was run over by a car, leaving behind a wife and three young children. I had often imagined what it would have been like to grow up without a father, yearning for his presence, and feeling short changed for having no memory of him. Even worse, I couldn't fathom being my great-grandmother at that time, raising three children under the age of seven, on her own, while dealing with the devastating loss of her husband. It captured my interest, as stories like this often do, and I was determined to know more.

I found a newspaper article from 1924 that described my great grandfather's accident. The article made the event become more than just a morbid fascination; it made the people involved *real* to me and I started to connect like I hadn't before. The article stated that a man had hit Robert and had not stopped "until two tires had run over his body." An ambulance was called to the scene, and Robert was rushed to the hospital, but he died while surgeons were working to repair his tattered body. The driver of the car mistakenly identified Robert as someone else, as a neighbor he knew, and the body was taken to the morgue to be cataloged under that neighbor's name. When Robert did not arrive home nearly 30 minutes after his expected time, my great-grandmother became concerned and called the police. They told her that a bicyclist had died, but not one named Robert Rodwell. She immediately called the morgue and the attendant repeated the story the police had relayed to her. She told the attendant that, if the man brought in were her husband, he would find his name written on the inside pocket of his jacket. The attendant checked and confirmed that the man was, in fact, Robert Rodwell. According to the newspaper, my great-grandmother "collapsed."

I cried for the first time, though I had heard an abridged version of the story in Grandma Rose's words many times. In reading this article, Robert was no longer just my great-grandfather with a sad past, who I never knew. He was slowly becoming someone who shaped my grandmother's life, as well as those who came after, in ways I had not understood. I became passionate about researching Robert's past, his family's stories, our family's roots. My passion became an obsession. My obsession…well…my obsession led to one of the greatest adventures of my life.

I truly believe that loved ones were working that summer to have their stories be known and told. They wanted me to know the details of events that were beyond their control, and they wanted me to know of their choices in reaction to those events which shaped their lives, and ultimately ours. There is no other explanation for how things came to pass when opening those boxes. There is no other explanation for how their legacies finally surfaced, so many years past their deaths.

Grandma Rose (middle) with her brothers, July 1924, three months after their father's accident

CYCLIST FATALLY HURT, AND DRIVER OF CAR ARRESTED

Dzadula, in Borrowed Car, Hits Robert L. Rodwell, Solvay Plant Worker.

HELD IN $2,000 BAIL

Vernon Howe, 15, Professor's Son, Accused of Fleeing After Felling Man.

Stanley J. Dzadula, 316 Wilkinson Street, driver of the automobile which struck and killed Robert L. Rodwell, 37, of 155 Coolidge Avenue, last night, today was ordered held in $2,000 bail on a charge of reckless driving following an inquest by Coroner Crane. It was said the charge may be changed to *[illegible]* after other witnesses are examined.

One other person is under arrest as a result of yesterday's auto accidents, Vernon Howe, 15, son of a Syracuse University professor, Frank W. Howe, 649 East Colvin Street. The boy was operating the car which ran down Peter Zaleski, 107 Tioga Street, in Otisco Street and sped away without stopping.

Victim Riding Bicycle.

Rodwell, shift foreman in the employ of the Solvay Process Company, was riding his bicycle at West Genesee and West Fayette Streets on his way home from work when the car driven by Dzadula knocked him from his bicycle.

George Fishbank, 205 Willis Avenue, and J. C. Ketcham, 824 West Onondaga Street, who testified at the Coroner's inquest this *[illegible]*

Fatally Injured When Hit by Auto

ROBERT L. RODWELL.

Newspaper article, detailing Robert Rodwell's death

JIM

JANUARY 17, 1944

Dear Rose,

My darling niece, when my brother died, I made a silent promise that I would help his children know the man he was by knowing me. It is difficult to keep that promise while I am away at war because I am no longer able to spend time with you. However, I can stay connected by writing letters to share my brother's legacy as well as sharing my own experiences and thoughts. I like to think that, if you know me, you will know your father and I hope my letters will be your link to him. For these reasons, this is the first of many letters you will receive from me, though I do not use the word "many" as an indication of hope for a long and drawn out war.

Steadfast and Loyal,
Uncle Jim

JANUARY 26, 1944

Dear Rose,

We arrived in England today. The trip was long, crowded, and fairly rough at sea, but we filled our time with card games, stories of home, and friendship. As they did in the last war, these journeys bring us closer as army brothers, and there is much to be said for that. The men in the army have become family to me and have helped to fill some of the void left from the loss of my parents and my brother, Robert.

Our arrival in England was at night. Blackout was in effect there, so the pier where we landed was virtually deserted except for the workers. On one of the many ramps at the ship's lower level, soldiers disembarked to find a thin board placed as a "welcome mat" on which to wipe their feet and stomp their boots; drawn on the board was the face of Hitler which quickly became unrecognizable beneath a mass of Army boot prints, Hitler's face stomped into obscurity. It was a fitting gesture of friendship from our British allies.

Carrying their packs, their bedrolls, and their excitement, GIs lined up to check in and receive supplies. Several Red Cross canteen girls stood with crates of donuts for the men while, further down the line, more volunteers stood to pass out packs of lifesavers, chewing gum, and chocolate. Meanwhile, other soldiers unloaded the ship of the crates full of rations, ammo, and supplies as vehicles were driven down ramps onto land. The ports were clogged with movement, the port cities overrun with activity.

Next, trains were boarded for the training camps, with more lines in which to wait. Once at their destination, the trains led to still more lines where men waited to board vehicles. These vehicles formed long convoys that carried soldiers and supplies through the English countryside.

We arrived at our designated camp and saw neat rows of tents that would serve as bunk houses, hospitals, and more. Enlisted soldiers unloaded crates from the convoy of vehicles and added these to mountainous, tarp covered supply piles containing enough supplies for the time we will spend in England, as well as stockpiling for the upcoming invasion. The Signal Corps worked to unwind reels of wire in order to create communication networks. Cooks set up outdoor kitchens. Mechanics tended to and refueled vehicles. Medics set up the hospital, dentist, and x-ray tents. The original hustle of the seaports was transferred here as soldiers made these tent cities operational.

When I left our regiment's area to be taken to Division Headquarters, I felt the excitement of the enlisted men, but I also thought about what was to come. I wondered if their wide-eyed naivety was the brain's way of sheltering the men who had not yet become hardened by war. Perhaps, subconsciously, their excitement acted as a protective cloud that blocked the realities of life they had yet to experience, and kept them from acknowledging their fears.

Still, I felt excited for them too, because they were just starting to form families of brothers who would become as close as (if not closer than) their actual families. They were at the first stop of their crossing over and, for now, they were out of harm's way. As I drove towards HQ, I smiled and said a silent prayer for the men in my regiment who were on the brink of a great journey.

Steadfast and Loyal,
Uncle Jim

TEDDY

MARCH 20, 1944
JOURNAL — TEDDY ROOSEVELT, JR.

I had finally received word that I should report to General Headquarters in England at once. A great weight had been lifted as this is all I have been asking for (and what I have been continuously denied) for months. I will be with the assault forces in the next phase of the war!

My travel lasted four days and four nights and the journey was horrendous. I was terribly ill with chest pains and an awful cough. At one point, the army doctor examining me said my fever had reached over one hundred three degrees. It was pneumonia (the chest pains from fluid in my lungs) and I was urged to go to a hospital. I refused. Nothing was going to block the success of my exhaustive efforts to join the fight!

Little did I know, the matter was out of my hands. When on the train to HQ, my aide, Stevie, called ahead for an ambulance and it was waiting for me at the station when I arrived. I spent three weeks in the hospital which was very frustrating, but at least it provided me with ample time to read, nothing seriously troubling my mind except my desire to reach my destination. Towards the end of my stay, though, reading was not enough to keep me content and the nurses needed to leave me alone. They coddled me. They patted me on the head, like a child. I could hardly stand it. I had seen nurses on the front who were covered in blood, their hair matted from sweat, their bodies covered in grime, who never treated soldiers that way. You would not see any of those nurses patting an old general on the head while he was recovering! I suppose I am being unfair to the nurses who took care of me over the course of those three weeks, but treating me as though I am an old man without a sound mind, irked me. Perhaps my edginess irked them just as much. Whatever the case, our time together needed to end.

When I finally escaped the nurses' pats and arrived at HQ, I was met by General Raymond O. Barton, affectionately nicknamed "Tubby." He has since told me how apprehensive he was of my transfer. He was worried that a President's son might be quite pretentious and conceited. (Will I never escape my father's shadow?) Thank goodness Tubby quickly shed his preconceived notions of me. What a fine man he is. He leads with integrity, trusts his officers (who are very well trained), and supports his men without holding his rank above their humanity. He seems to understand my leadership style and I appreciate that he lets me command the way I am most comfortable. Before this transfer, I was heartbroken to leave the 1st Infantry Division, but I have found a home with the 4th Infantry Division now. The loyalty and sense of comradery is the same as I experienced with the 1st Infantry Division, which makes me very content.

UNPACKING YESTERDAY | 7

Original copy of now famous picture of Teddy Roosevelt, Jr., found among Uncle Jim's mementos. (Notice the bullet hole in the windshield.)

JIM

MARCH 24, 1944

Dear Rose,

I don't know if I told you about meeting the son of President Theodore Roosevelt. He was formally named Theodore, after his father, but he goes by Ted. The soldiers call him "General Teddy." He is a Brigadier General and we work in close proximity under General Barton. We had met back in '41 during the Carolina Maneuvers, but he was part of the 1st Infantry Division then. It is the 4th Infantry Division's good fortune that he was transferred here, and he is an asset to our unit.

Ted is short in stature, but certainly not short in spirit. His face is deeply lined (marks of his joyful disposition) and his round eyes rest within his wink-lines. When he flashes his wide grin, his mood is instantly contagious and all the men light up when he comes around. He gets around with the aid of a cane which seems to act like an additional appendage, embellishing his already larger-than-life personality. He often salutes, using his cane, and we have to duck or quickly remove ourselves from his general area so as not to become injured! He also uses his cane to bat men away if they try to help him maneuver, making sure no one perceives him as being in need of special treatment. When I see Ted, trudging along with one of his canes, inspecting the troops or joking around, it makes me smile with my whole being.

I was immediately drawn to Ted, and we have become fast friends. We have spent much of our leisure time sharing stories of home. Though his area of New York (Oyster Bay) is far from ours, his tales still bring me back to the place of my childhood. Being close to Ted makes me feel close to the family I have lost, and to you, my dear niece. It fills my heart with a sense of peace.

Steadfast and Loyal,
Uncle Jim

 **Beth Rieman** is in Mentor, Ohio.
August 3, 2018 at 12:00 PM • Mentor, OH •

Uncle Jim's dress medals

I remember how much my Grandma Rose treasured her uncle's dress medals from WWII. She showed them to my brother and me when we were too young to understand their significance, and when neither of us showed much interest, she put them away to be shared again when we were older. Well, I am interested now and I am sitting here in awe after spending the evening searching online for matching pictures in order to identify each medal. The first medal on the left is a Distinguished Service Cross! This is a huge deal, second only to the Medal of Honor! The next is a Silver Star (the oak leaf cluster on its ribbon indicates a second Silver Star)! There is a Legion of Honor, a Bronze Star with an oak leaf cluster, the Croix de Guerre from French Royalty…WOW! Uncle Jim must have been very brave and valiant!

Knowing that Uncle Jim touched these and wore them on his uniform, that he was proud of them and passed them on for someone in his family to cherish, is just incredible to me. I am disappointed in myself for being uninterested in the past because I now believe it is important to know about the people who made us who we are. I believe we have a responsibility to know family members' stories and keep the stories alive when loved ones are gone. Since Uncle Jim had no children of his own, I feel a strong pull on my heart to make sure his stories are not lost, that his legacy continues. And I have a feeling this is just the beginning. Tomorrow, my dad is going to get my grandma's boxes out of storage so that we can open them and, hopefully, find some family stories inside.

JIM

MARCH 26, 1944

Dear Rose,

Being in England, I have become very aware of how different it is to be someone living in Europe than it is to live in America. Both countries are at war, but our daily lives are affected very differently. In the States, you are feeling the effects of war but it is still far away from you. You are rationing; you are doing without in order to support the war effort, and you are missing family members who are serving, but England is different.

The British people have been through so much more than we have. They have been at war since 1939 and their towns reflect the toll the five years have taken. Houses are not painted because their factories are focused on military production. The trains here have no heat because power is conserved for use in the factories. Community parks have been turned into gardens for growing vegetables. There are blackouts every night, for the entire night. Even soap is scarce in England. The people here have had their homes destroyed, their family members killed, and their incomes severely taxed. Americans are living in a country that is at war, but England is also living in a war zone.

We are in Tiverton which is a small town that sits on the juncture of two rivers, with an old Norman castle, an ornately detailed 16th century church, and a remarkable town hall that towers in the center of the city. Just beyond the city, on one of the rivers is a place named "Collipriest House" which is part of a large estate that seems untouched by the war. The house belongs to a family and is typically used as a summer home, I believe, but now it is being used as our division headquarters. I have not learned any details regarding the family who gave up their home for us, but we are grateful to use it as our temporary home now.

After entering the gated entrance to Collipriest, narrow roads on the estate grounds wind past groupings of beech trees, around open pastures through which the river runs, and make their way to the house which is built to appear as if it is tucked into a hillside of trees. Every room of the three-story home has 12-paned windows lining each wall, affording views from each vantage point. The house and the entire estate are quite grand.

The army's daily maneuvers and trainings take place in an area away from this estate, so the evenings have offered a respite from rising nerves over our imminent assault. Ted and I, as well as some of the more "seasoned" officers, have enjoyed fishing for trout in the river and spending time indoors with some whiskey, sharing stories of our previous war experiences. At Collipriest, we feel far away from battle preparation and planning. It is deceptively peaceful here—a stretch of calm on the outskirts of war.

Being in England makes me think of my father (your grandfather) quite often. I don't know if you know that he came from England before Robert and I were born. What it must have been like to leave England, set sail across the same ocean I crossed, and start over in a new country! I am filled with pride when I think of the choices my father made, the obstacles he overcame, and the life he made for himself, the life he made for all of us. Rose, your grandfather was brave, determined, and strong. If only he weren't taken from us too soon.

I know that you and I share many understandings when it comes to losing a parent. I lost my mother on my first birthday so I understand how it feels to long for a relationship with a parent who departed unfamiliar. I lost my father when I was seven years old so I understand how it feels to spend your life without a father playing a role in it.

I know that you feel the same emotions, and I know you wish for just one memory, any memory, to hold in your heart. Suddenly orphans, Robert and I were sent to live with an aunt in Connecticut, and we spent our entire childhoods with a fixed determination to find our way back to the town of our births. Though we had only lived there as young children, it was the only place that felt like home to us, and we longed to be in the place that held memories born of our parents' love. You are blessed to have one parent still, and a childhood spent in a home where your father's affection could still be felt, even after he passed.

I share these things as part of my promise to help you know our father's legacy, and mine as well. I have had a lot of sadness in my life, but it has helped me become the soldier I am, and the leader I have risen to be. That sadness simmers, deep within me, and develops into the courage I use to push myself forward, to protect my men, and to succeed at all costs. Your father showed me that sadness can be turned into tenacity. I hope you are able to use your own sadness to help you persevere, just as your father and grandfather and I have done. You come from the most resilient stock, Rose. You are a Rodwell and our legacy will live on through you.

Steadfast and Loyal,
Uncle Jim

P.S. Have you wondered why I always sign off with "Steadfast and Loyal"? This is the motto of the 4th Infantry Division. I love the motto for our division, but I also love it for life in general, and for our uncle/niece relationship. It seems fitting in so many ways.

A picture of the 4th Division headquarters in England, "Collipriest House," found in Uncle Jim's scrapbook

TEDDY

MARCH 28, 1944
JOURNAL — TEDDY ROOSEVELT, JR.

I have a few aides, but Lt. Marcus O. Stevenson, nicknamed "Stevie," is one of my favorites. He is from Texas, with a southern accent and a mustache that you would expect to see on a cowboy. It fits. Stevie is my "right-hand man" and he has been with me since the start of this war, back when I was with the 1st Infantry Division in the Mediterranean; he transferred with me to the 4th Infantry Division. Stevie hands me my cane when I need it, gathers my belongings, keeps my pistol clean and ready, drives me from place to place, and so much more. He also attempts to keep me in line with military expectations, although, through no fault of Stevie's, I often fall short. For example, he tries to get me to tidy my appearance, but I will never see the point in sprucing up while preparing to go to war so I don't put in the effort (It is not as if I am going to march in a parade). He is also relentless in encouraging me to wear my army issued helmet. I hate my helmet. It is uncomfortable and ridiculously cumbersome. When he gives it to me, I usually toss it into the back of the jeep—where it belongs. I often get reprimanded by superiors for not wearing it, though, so Stevie keeps handing me the darned thing. I suppose Stevie's hope springs eternal.

Stevie stenciled the words "Rough Rider" on the windshield of my jeep as homage to my father's war service. Originally, I was a bit embarrassed by it, but I know that it was painted as a gesture of kindness, and it has since grown on me, becoming part of my identity now. Just below the words, in the middle of the windshield, there is a bullet hole that I have kept unpatched. When Stevie and I are making the rounds in the jeep, I am often asked how the bullet hole got there. I always say, "Stevie was trying to commit suicide, but he didn't know how." Stevie rolls his eyes because he has heard it so many times, but the joke is always met with smiles from the soldiers. (I think, secretly, Stevie likes all my wise cracks, and would be lost without them.)

In all seriousness, Stevie is like family to me. I am grateful for all he does and I am very fond of him (even if he is an abysmal failure at keeping his Brigadier General in line).

JIM

APRIL 1, 1944

Dear Rose,

Our Commanding General, General Raymond O. Barton (who we all call "Tubby") is someone I have known for a long time now. I actually met him in 1917 when I joined the Plattsburg Training Camp in New York (the National Officer Candidate School); he was a captain and I was an officer candidate in the field artillery battery. In the first great war, we crossed paths when I was returning home a captain after serving in the 2nd Cavalry overseas and Tubby was leaving the States to command the 1st Battalion of the 8th Infantry Regiment during the postwar occupation. He also spent a year as the Chief of Staff for the 4th Division (the job I hold now) so he understands my daily responsibilities. All of this makes us closer as we have a deeper understanding through shared experiences, but I think we would have been close regardless.

When he was at West Point, he was a heavyweight wrestler which earned him the nickname "Tubby." He is certainly not fat or even round, but the nickname has stuck. He has a short, clipped mustache, and his face is weathered by age and responsibility. His expression is most often contemplative, frequently consumed by thoughts that cover many things at once. He has a reputation for being a strict disciplinarian, but not in a grizzly way; he commands with an iron fist because what lies ahead of us is not something to be taken lightly and he wants us to be well prepared. He puts our division through exhaustive training, but he is also always present for the trainings, moving among the ranks every day. The men respect his leadership and want to make him proud. When we began training in the States, he told the men, "90% of you will cooperate… I'll take care of the other 10%." Needless to say, no one wants to be part of that other 10%.

When you move past Tubby's strict approach, what you also find is a general who cares deeply about the men he leads. He puts the men first and would risk his rank to argue on their behalf. He is very revered and also loved. I would be surprised if you can find a soldier who feels otherwise. Personally, I hold him in the highest esteem and have a fierce loyalty for him. I consider it an honor to be serving under his command.

Steadfast and Loyal,
Uncle Jim

UNPACKING YESTERDAY | 21

Uncle Jim and General Barton, October 1943, while still in the States, picture found in Uncle Jim's scrapbook

TEDDY

APRIL 2, 1944
JOURNAL — TEDDY ROOSEVELT, JR.

I have completely settled into the 4th Infantry Division and I am happier than I expected. I really enjoy this group of men, the officers, and Tubby Barton. I have a home here with the 4th Infantry Division, which I was not sure I would find after transferring. A tank battalion was added to my command, one that had been with me in Sicily, so I also have a bit of my beloved 1st Infantry Division with me as well. I am grateful.

It is nice to talk with a few men who fought in the last war and compare stories. Roddy (that is what we call him, a nickname that is a play on his surname, Rodwell) was in Germany in the last war and led the cavalry to the front while I was in France with the 26th Infantry Regiment of the 1st Infantry Division.

It is odd to think that we are both heading back to the same places in which we fought to do it all over again, battling tyranny with democracy. This time, I will be heading there with the use of a cane, which I suppose is rather ironic, since I left the last war in a stretcher. I wonder how close our fighting will be to Soissons. Wouldn't it be ironic to be back in the very spot where I was shot.

That bullet went right through, above and behind my knee, leaving two holes. I was irritated because it caused my removal from action. I refused to have them care for me the day I was shot (other than an anti-tetanus and a bandage), and I kept fighting, but they still removed me. I was sent home like an invalid with a sign attached to my shirt that read, "Gunshot Wound Severe," and the sign caused everyone at home to fuss, telling me I needed to go to the hospital. I just wanted a shower, a good dinner, and a place to rest my feet. I wouldn't let Bunny tend to the wound, even though she insisted it was her obligation as both my wife and a Red Cross volunteer. I simply wanted a clean bandage and to be left alone.

That was until my brother-in-law, Dick, arrived. He was the chief surgeon of the 2nd Infantry Division and insisted on looking at it. He told me my wound was full of dirt and pieces of cloth, and that my leg seemed to be paralyzed. He said the bullet went through an area where important tendons, nerves, and veins ran through my leg. If it was not cleaned immediately, he told me, it would become infected and I could lose my leg. That made me acquiesce and I was taken to the hospital for surgery. Fortunately, the surgeon was able to clean the wound and stitch it up. My leg was not amputated, but I have not had any feeling in my heel since. I think Dick most likely saved my leg by forcing me to stop being so stubborn. I was in the hospital for two days and then sent home to recover.

Eventually, my leg was put in a metal splint and I was given crutches to help me walk. It was the most unpleasant experience of my life, because I wanted to get back to my men and return to the front. General Summerall assured me in writing, "I think no one who has been a member of this Division occupies a higher place than you in the esteem of your comrades, and you will receive a warm welcome whenever it shall be our good fortune to have you return to us." This was very kind and brought tears to my eyes, but I just wanted to be cleared for duty, quickly. On my thirty-first birthday, I went to teach at the Army Line School while entering the General Staff College for my own training, and I did so without crutches, only with the use of a cane. I was anxious to get back to France, and was sure I would be there soon, but the war ended shortly after and so did my war service.

I already had severe arthritis in my hip prior to the war, and now, coupled with the shot to my knee, I need to use a cane permanently. I have resigned myself to that, as I could have faced a worse outcome. Therefore, I am always prepared and keep more than one cane with me, especially if I am far from home. I would not want to have just one cane in my possession and, in battle or otherwise, have it damaged beyond use. I would have to wait for a replacement to be made or try to find a shop for purchasing a new cane, which at war, would be close to impossible. So, I make sure to have at least one trench cane and a typical walking cane with me when I travel. Stevie is good to keep track of my canes and he always has them ready to pass to me, a cane being a necessary extra limb to me now. One could say that Teddy Roosevelt and his walking stick go together like biscuits and gravy!

JIM

APRIL 10, 1944

Dear Rose,

Together, Ted and I are the right combination of sarcastic (me) and playful (he) which makes us a believable team when we want to have a little fun around camp. We used our "teamwork" to have a little fun with some of the "greener" privates today...

After mess, I pretended to be sick. I was subtle at first, casually interjecting my feelings of discomfort into the conversation as Ted and I spoke with a group of enlisted men. Then I allowed it to escalate and made it seem as though I could vomit at any moment. Suddenly, I quickly reached for anything nearby in which to get sick, but pretended as though I couldn't find anything. So, Ted, playing up a sense of urgency and concern, grabbed the first thing he could find on the table: his helmet (in which we had secretly stashed a little of our evening's food). I turned my back on the men and pretended to vomit in the helmet, returned with the helmet in my hands, wiped my mouth, and then placed the helmet on the ground. We "ignored" the incident, so as not to embarrass anyone, and we moved the conversation along.

Then Ted casually picked up the helmet mid-sentence, removed a fork from his pocket while finishing his sentence, and started eating from the "vomit" filled helmet. The men were completely repulsed. Ted just grinned a mischievous grin, chomping his teeth and smacking his lips, until they all realized they were just pranked. What a hoot!

I adore Ted. He has become such a close friend in such a short period of time. He fills my soul with joy.

Steadfast and Loyal,
Uncle Jim

Beth Rieman is in Mentor, Ohio
August 5, 2018 at 12:00 pm • Mentor, OH

What treasures we found today—an entire scrapbook of newspaper clippings from WWII! Aunt Polly, Uncle Jim's wife, diligently collected any and all articles written about the 4th Infantry Division and glued them to the pages of a large album that has the 4th Infantry Division's ivy insignia on the front. It is going to take quite a while to read each article, but it is all there…battle details, names, pictures of the places Uncle Jim had been. During WWII, I imagine reading the newspaper and finding details of a particular division brought comfort to the people back home. Mail traveled slowly and sometimes there was no contact at all, during periods of time when mail was not allowed to come in and out of the areas in which men were stationed. I think I would have been scouring the pages of the papers every day too, but Aunt Polly went one step further. She kept the articles and organized them. She was clearly proud of her husband's service and wanted his legacy to be shared.

JIM

APRIL 20, 1944

Dear Rose,

As we continue to ready ourselves for the great invasion, I am filled with thoughts of my father. I assume you do not know much about him, or my mother for that matter, as you would not have grown up hearing your father tell stories of his parents. I am not sure your mother even knows the details to share with you. Quite honestly, I know very little, as both parents were taken from Robert and me when we were so very young, but I want you to know your lineage so that your family will know the people who came before them.

My father (your grandfather), William Rodwell, came from Lincolnshire, England, in 1870. He was a hard-working, industrious man, coming to America with no possessions, and passing from this earth having acquired a farm of 70 acres, including vast orchards, a house, outbuildings, and an evaporator. Our home was in Clyde, New York in an area called, "Hunt's Corners." My father ran the first steam-thresher in the county for eighteen years. Later, my father owned a peppermint distillery, having realized that there was something in the soil in Clyde that made peppermint grow plentifully. My father was well liked, even loved, by the people who knew him, and he and my mother, Flora (Helen was her given name), often entertained large groups of guests in their home. When they were married in 1894, they had over one hundred people at their home to celebrate.

I am not sure how our parents met, but I do know that my mother had been a school teacher for thirteen years before marrying, and I know our farm was just over a mile east of the school house. I imagine my parents would have crossed paths a number of times. My mother's family, the Woodworth family, is an old, established family, with many direct ancestral lines to grandfathers who fought in the Revolutionary war, as well as lines tracing back to the Mayflower. With their marriage, my mother's heritage and my father's success must have made for a union in town that was admired.

I know, from the memories I do have, that my father was heartbroken when my mother passed away. I don't think she was ill for a long time, and I don't know how she died, though I know it was something to do with her heart. I was too young to ask those questions when my father was alive, and Robert was as well.

When my mother died, our older cousin, Maude, came to live with us for a time, to help my father who was lost having to learn to do the things my mother had done. I was just one year old, Robert only three. I can't imagine how my father could have handled his responsibilities as a farmer and business owner in addition to raising two young boys without Maude's help.

It was not long, though, before our father died in an accident. He was climbing a twenty-foot tall ladder to pick apples in the orchard, and he fell. He was found unconscious and taken to the hospital where doctors determined he was paralyzed from the fall. There were other complications as well and he died six months later in a convalescent home. Robert was nine years old; I was seven.

I remember my father as being firm, but also loving. We did not cross him, but we also knew to watch him closely because his behaviors would give clues about his mood, and there were many times that his serious nature would fade away. Then, Robert and I would climb on his back, chase him around the farm fields, and play hide-and-seek in the orchards.

Even without our mother, our father made our house feel warm and we always felt loved. We loved when it was time to harvest the apples because there was so much activity at the house, and we were allowed to help. However, our favorite time of year was winter because our father would not be as burdened with farm work. Some days, he would tie a wooden pallet to one of our horses, and allow us to sit on it while the horse pulled us, racing through the snow-covered fields. Then he would build a fire inside the house and he would read stories to us while we warmed our frozen toes, feeling completely happy.

I hate the snow now. I suppose, with the snow, come memories that are difficult to revisit.

Growing up without a father or a mother was often heart wrenching. I was envious of other children who had intact families. I never had a chance to feel a mother's love, at least not in a way I could remember. And losing our father was devastating because, at that point, we were old enough to understand. When he died, we were appointed a guardian and the family farm was sold at auction. We were homeless and orphaned so we were sent to live in Connecticut, where we felt ripped from the only place our parents' feet had touched the ground. We returned to Clyde as soon as Robert was old enough to be considered my guardian, his senior year in high school. We found a boarding house, and shared a room there, and although it was not an intact family, it felt like we had finally come home. That was when Robert fell in love with your mother too. It was a good time in our lives.

Seven years later, Robert was gone.

I pray each night and I believe there is a heaven. I have to believe I will be reunited with my mother, my father, and Robert someday. I was not given enough time with any of them here on earth, so it has to exist. It is too difficult to think otherwise. In the present, I just hope I am making all of them proud. I want them all to be looking down on me and smiling.

   Steadfast and Loyal,
   Uncle Jim

TEDDY

APRIL 23, 1944
JOURNAL — TEDDY ROOSEVELT, JR.

It is challenging to be the son of an adored American President, and even more so as his namesake. In politics, I have always fallen a bit short. In personality, I am somewhat dwarfed. In tenacity, my tales are not as bold. I often feel like I cannot find the sun for my father's shadow, but I also want to be just like him. It is the great conundrum of my life.

Growing up, I couldn't help but idolize my father. He was larger than life, with a magnetism even his biggest critics couldn't deny. He drew people in and ignited their passions. He made dramatic entrances and loved the press corps; his boisterous personality charmed them all. He was a man of honor and strength and character. I have always had great respect, admiration, and love for my father. Standing only 5'9" tall, he was a giant of a man.

He was a demanding father but also warm and funny. His expectations could be overpowering at times, but even with his aggressively competitive nature, he was also very tenderhearted and kind. We loved our father's company and he gave us a childhood of outdoor adventures that included hunting, expeditions, pony riding, camping, games, and more. My father loved to joke and his hearty laugh seemed to take over his entire body, flushing his cheeks, changing the pitch of his voice, bringing tears to his eyes. When one of us was the cause of that laughter, we felt like we had won a championship.

My father was the most interesting man I have ever known, with so many diverse experiences crammed into his sixty years of life. He overcame a nearly fatal childhood illness by engaging in rigorous fitness, which led to competitive boxing and wrestling in college, and a love for daily exercise his entire life. He graduated magna cum laude from Harvard and wrote thirty-eight books in his lifetime. He was, among other things, a member of the New York assembly, the Assistant Secretary of the Navy, the Colonel of the Rough Riders, the Governor of New York, the Vice President of the United States and the President of the United States. In addition to politics, he was a founding member of the National Institute of the Arts and was recognized in the scientific community as a leading paleontologist, ornithologist, and taxidermist. He was a big game collector for the Smithsonian. All of this and he managed to read 1-3 books per day, recite poetry, and be an attentive father to all of his children. (I am tired just from listing all of this, yet he lived it!)

One of the many things my father passed onto his children was his respect for the military. He had grown up hearing his mother tell her brothers' Civil War stories, he read books about war, he became the world's expert on the Naval War of 1812, and he entered the service as well, now famous for being the Colonel of the Rough Riders. From a very young age, he felt a desire to emulate the great soldiers of the past and he believed wars were won by the mental courage of men who were great thinkers.

To the same degree that I adored my father, he also adored his own. He looked up to his father for his business success and philanthropic contributions. His father was a wealthy businessman who also helped to found the American Museum of Natural History and the Metropolitan Museum of Art. My father admitted that he did not make any decisions throughout his presidency without considering what his father might have done; he thought very highly of his father's intelligence.

Yet, my father was also at odds with the respect he had for his father and the shame he felt over a specific choice his father made that tarnished his character. It was complicated growing up in my father's home. His father was a proud New Yorker and was loyal to the Union, his beliefs aligning with Lincoln's. His mother, on the other hand, was a southern belle who never lost her affection for the Confederacy. When the Civil War began, she begged her husband to not join a war that would encourage a fight against her southern brothers, dividing their household. He appeased his wife and hired a $300 substitute to serve in his place.

His father tried to eradicate his guilt by promoting the Union cause, but the damage had been done in his son's eyes. My father never overcame the disappointment he felt over his father's choice. He watched family friends fight, and even die in the war, and he was embarrassed to have a father who would use his wealth to avoid military service. Consequently, my father brought us up to believe that if we lived to see a war, we needed to ensure we would be able to explain to our children the reasons why we joined the front, rather than explaining why we didn't. This was at the heart of my father's desire to instill militarism in his children, and he was very proud to have all four of his sons enlist in the last great war. He spent his life atoning his own father's guilt and we were also quick to right the wrong.

Like my father, I graduated from Harvard. I was elected to the New York state assembly. I was Undersecretary of the Navy. Like my father, I am an outdoorsman and I have collected specimens for museums. I share my father's literary qualities as an author and I also served as Vice President of a publishing house. I equally enjoy reciting poetry and I believe a day is not complete without some good-natured joking and a lot of laughing. Unlike my father, I was defeated in my race for New York

Governor, but the political aspiration was the same. I have experienced success professionally and financially, but at a very young age, I knew I wanted to be an officer in the military. This is the career to which I feel I am best suited. I tried my hand in politics, but military leadership is to me what the political scene was to my father. It is where I feel the most pulled and what I love doing.

For good reason, I am constantly compared to my father, and I am not blind to the parallels, but I struggle to forge my own trail and rise to the level of honor that comes packaged in the name I bear. I have been determined to earn my father's pride my entire life, and I hope that, one day, I will become a man of the same caliber my father was.

I carry a letter my father wrote to me, one of the last penned before his death. It has become worn from my handling, one of my most treasured possessions. In part, he wrote in regard to my military service, "I'm so proud of you. You have won high honor, not only for your children, but like the Chinese, you have ennobled your ancestors. I walk with my head higher because of you."

I hope so, Father, I do so hope I make you proud.

President Roosevelt's family, Teddy standing, far right (Library of Congress)

JIM

MAY 1, 1944

Dear Rose,

I know this means you will be receiving melancholy letters, twice in a row, but I have been thinking about Robert. We have spoken about him many times throughout your life, but I am not sure I have ever written about him. Perhaps this is a letter you can look back on when you are feeling sad about his loss. Perhaps it can help you to know him better. Perhaps it is just a letter I needed to write to somehow make my words permanent, so that the details, and his memory, are not lost.

The day I received the telegram from your mother and read the words, "accident" and "gone," my life changed in an instant. I felt an immediate sense of abandonment. I lost the one remaining person who knew me as a child. I lost the only person who knew what it was like to grow up having lost both parents, longing for their return, longing to remain in our childhood home. Robert was supposed to walk this earth with me longer than anyone else I knew, and now, just like all the members of my immediate family, he was gone. And I was alone. Completely alone.

After reading the telegram, I was in a fog. Nothing was as it had been. I don't even remember much of the next few hours, but I know that I sprang into action. I was given three weeks leave of absence from

Fort Ringgold on the Texas border and I rode four hundred miles in a flivver roadster loaned to me by the army. When I reached San Antonio, I boarded an army plane for New York. Rain and fog, however, forced us to land in Oklahoma, at which point, I found a train to take me the rest of the way. I didn't realize how much of a trip it was until we were well underway, and all the delays made it feel like I was racing against time. Your mother postponed the funeral so that I could be there to help with the arrangements, to support her, and to say goodbye to my brother.

When I got to New York, and came to your home, the house was full of Robert. One of his coats hung on a hook near the door. His shaving supplies were still in the bathroom. Even you, his children, were reflections of him. Memories of my brother were scattered in every corner of your house.

Your mother's pain was visible. I had lost my dear brother, but she had lost her life partner, the father of her children, the man with whom she was supposed to grow old. She now had three very young children to raise on her own. I don't know how that would have felt: the shock and grief of such a devastating loss compounded with the reality of being left to parent alone and to grow old alone. It occurs to me, as I write this, that your mother felt what my father must have felt when he was a widower. I often marvel at your mother's strength, how she was able to carry on for the three of you and make a loving home that still honored your father, refusing to take another husband while you were growing up. What a testament to your parents' love and to your mother's character.

I love your mother and she is my sister, if not biologically, then certainly emotionally. I had already been very close to her while Robert was living, but his death brought us closer. We are the only two people alive who knew Robert to the depths only a brother and wife can. We have clung to that. She had to be strong for all of you, but she didn't need to do the same for me. We were able to grieve together. This helped close the distance between Robert and Robert's absence.

Before all of this, my life and Robert's always seemed to fall into two categories: before our parents' deaths, and after their deaths. Now life was marked by the same categories, but with Robert's name attached. Before—when Robert was alive. After—when life somehow had to continue without him. For everyone else, the world kept turning, but my world had stopped. I felt so shattered. I was missing a part of me. Like an amputee misses a limb, Robert had been cut from my body. Every morning, I woke up to realize that limb was still missing. I had to hobble through life without him. And I didn't want to. I still don't want to.

Yet, every day, brief mental snapshots of him come to me at the most unexpected times and they fill me with such joy. A memory of him, six years old, my big brother, cocking his head to one side and bending down, just under my chin, in order to smile up at me while he offers an apple from our orchard, in Clyde. A moment remembered when he was hugging me as we fell asleep, young boys, just nine and seven years old, lost and displaced without our parents, in a strange new Connecticut home. An image of when we were finally old enough to come back to Clyde, Robert acting as my guardian though only two years my senior—the look on his face when we settled into the boarding house and we knew we were finally home. Remembering how he would toss the football to me after school and how he came to every one of my high school games, acting as a father would (he had to grow up so fast). A vivid memory of when I was walking by the Clyde River with Robert and your mother, watching them fall in love, the sun dancing on Robert's skin, instantly turning his complexion dark, your mother flirting with him, the smile on her face giving away her feelings.

Rose, you have your father's eyes, which are our mother's (your grandmother's); this means you have my eyes too. You have his skin, skin that tans so quickly and holds such a beautiful color. You have his love for reading books, devouring stories, and becoming lost in them. He would have been proud of the woman you have become, just as I am proud of you.

Being able to be part of your life and watching you grow up has given me small pieces of my lost brother, but it still is sometimes a painful reminder that he is not here. Not only have I lost Robert, but I lost the role he would have played in the future, and so have all of you. Every event in life since his death brings to light the fact that he is not there to experience it. No matter how happy the occasion, there is a bittersweet undercurrent. I cannot share moments with him, and I long to do so. (I know you feel this way too). However, at some point, I realized I had to go on without Robert. And I had to keep him alive as best as I could without his physical presence. I had to make sure his essence was not lost.

That is when I promised I would help you know your father by letting you know me. I would share memories of him while also sharing my stories with you. In knowing me, you know him, because we were interconnected, like roots underground that you cannot see, roots that grow together in a pattern that turns in harmonious array, giving life to what you see above ground. This comforts me. This brings me peace. I hope it offers a little of the same for you, my dear niece.

Steadfast and Loyal,
Uncle Jim

Robert Rodwell, WWI

RODE 400 MILES IN FLIVVER, THEN BEGAN AIR DASH

Capt. Rodwell, Here for Brother's Funeral, Tells of Race From Texas.

Captain James S. Rodwell rode 400 miles in a rickety flivver before he reached San Antonio Tuesday to embark in an airplane waiting to carry him to Syracuse for the funeral of his brother, Robert L. Rodwell, victim of an accident.

He arrived in Syracuse Friday and attended the funeral yesterday, coming from Muskogee, Okla., by train after rain and fog had forced the plane down. An army aviator piloted the airplane in the transcontinental race against time.

"I received the telegram from my sister-in-law Tuesday, got three weeks leave of absence from Fort Renggold on the Texas border and rode in a flivver roadster to San Antonio. I didn't realize how much of a trip it was until we were well under way." Captain Rodwell said. He will help Mrs. Rodwell in arranging her affairs following the sudden death of her husband.

1924 Newspaper article, detailing Uncle Jim's race against time

TEDDY

MAY 2, 1944
JOURNAL — TEDDY ROOSEVELT, JR.

Last night, Roddy was not quite himself when we sat for dinner at HQ. He was seemingly withdrawn, something heavy on his heart. After mess, we walked for a time, and he shared his thoughts, thoughts of the brother he had lost, and the family before that. Roddy has experienced a lot of sadness in his lifetime. It made me think of my own losses, and I realize now that sharing similar experiences with Roddy brings us closer as army brothers.

I think the only thing that saved me, when my brother Quentin died, was being a father and having to focus on my own family while grieving. Soon after, I was also given a gift with the birth of our third son, whom Bunny and I named Quentin in my brother's honor. He was born sixteen months after my brother's death and it gave new purpose. I have enjoyed watching my youngest son grow to be a tribute to his namesake.

Still, losing my brother was a very dark time in my life. And, being the son of a President, I couldn't escape it, not even for a moment. Quentin's death was splashed across newspaper headlines. Quentin's death was talked about in circles throughout America, in France, and likely other countries as well. It seems everyone admired Quentin, that he would give up a life of privilege and face the dangers of war. Even the Germans seemed moved by this, and gave Quentin, the man they had shot down in battle, a burial with full military honors. People around the world were mourning my brother's death, and it was hard for me to cope when surrounded by all of that, unable to grieve myself when the letters of sympathy poured in, when people who didn't even know Quentin tried to grieve with the rest of us.

Upon receipt of the telegram from the Red Cross, my parents rowed to the middle of Oyster Bay, alone, and stayed there for quite a while to mourn in private. Like me, I don't think they could find the space to process through Quentin's death, without being under a microscope, without having to pretend to be strong for everyone else. What that must have been like, floating on the water, sharing their broken hearts. Quentin's death was marked on the faces of my grief-stricken parents, and the shock of burying a son aged them almost instantly.

My mother, who tucked Quentin into bed the night before he left for war (a grown man still pampered by his mother's love) would read Quentin's last letters over and over again. She searched, trying to find peace in his words that reveled in the great adventure he was having in the war, letters that expressed his love for flying. She searched for comfort, knowing that he wanted to be in the war, that he loved being there, and that he died a noble death.

My father, the man who had previously dealt with the death of his first wife and his mother on the same day and in the same house, who had survived an assassination attempt, and who fought in the Spanish-American war, never recovered from the loss of Quentin, his youngest son. He would walk down to the stables, to the horses my brother loved dearly as a child, and he would just stand there, lost, whispering my brother's nickname, "Quenty-Quee," over and over again.

My father's once boisterous personality was immediately subdued and his health began to quickly decline. He died of a heart attack in his sleep six months later.

Quentin Roosevelt, Teddy's brother, 1917

JIM

MAY 13, 1944

Dear Rose,

We had a good laugh at our meeting today. The government has issued a handbook for all soldiers that outlines what a soldier should do in the event he is taken as a prisoner by the enemy. While I understand the necessity for training our men in anticipation of this outcome, the verbiage in the pamphlet is quite comical.

There is important information contained in the document, to be sure. In the event they are taken prisoner, men are told to only provide name, grade, and serial number, but nothing else. They are not to give the name of their unit or organization and are not make up false information either; just keep to the basics, give nothing else. They are told to forget everything they know about the army and to not trust anyone, even other prisoners, as they may be spies trying to gain information. This is all important.

However, the pages that discuss our "rights" are what I find to be humorous. Do we really believe the enemy is going to treat us as if we have any "rights" and adhere to the agreements of the Geneva Convention? Hitler is gassing Jews, killing anyone who confronts him, starving men, women, and children. How can we honestly think any German will treat captured American soldiers with courtesy?

For example, "Having been punished for an attempted escape, that attempt may not be held against you if you try to escape and are recaptured." (I am fairly certain that anyone caught escaping will be shot in the back of the head!)

Or—"If you are an officer, you may not be assigned to any work, except at your own request." (So, would they be giving me a comfortable place to rest, some books to read, maybe evening tea if I choose not to work?)

And the way the pamphlet is written (I suppose to boost morale) is hysterical—"If you do not ask for a copy of the Geneva Convention and read it, it is your own tough luck if certain rights are withheld from you." (Your own tough luck, do you hear me? Boy, that is funny!)

"Let the Geneva Convention be your Basic Field Manual while you are in captivity. Read it!" (This sounds like an Ovaltine advertisement)

I could go on and on for many pages, but I will leave you with the last page of the document—

> *"As a prisoner of war, you are in a tough spot, but—*
> *The army hasn't forgotten you—*
> *The Red Cross and The Protecting Power do all*
> *that they can for you—*
> *Your family and friends know where you are and*
> *will keep in touch with you—*
> *Your own pride as a soldier will pull you through."*

I am laughing so hard, I am crying. Tomorrow, I will hand these to the men and go over the details. I wonder if I can do so without laughing.

Steadfast and Loyal,
Uncle Jim

UNPACKING YESTERDAY | 53

Official handbook given to soldiers

TEDDY

MAY 15, 1944
JOURNAL — TEDDY ROOSEVELT, JR.

Until we are given orders to invade, we have no choice but to sit and wait. Our days are filled with briefings, meetings, drills, maneuvers, and trainings, but we all have a good deal of free time here as well. This leaves time to mingle with the people of England in their towns. Some of the families around here have also opened their homes and treat GIs to Sunday dinner; this has meant a lot to our boys who are missing many of the comforts of home, and they have formed some lasting friendships with their host families.

Many of the enlisted men have never left their home states, let alone crossed the ocean toward a foreign land. So, they were given handbooks titled "Instructions for American Servicemen in Britain" containing advice for mingling with the townspeople — from basic manners to explanations of cultural differences. They are told to be humble, to not talk too much, and to not assume British people are rude if they don't talk. There are some very direct statements, for example, "Don't make fun of British speech or accents. You sound just as funny to them but they are too polite to show it." Or, "Don't be misled by the British tendency to be soft-spoken and polite. If they need to be, they can be plenty tough. The English language didn't spread across the oceans and over the mountains and jungles and swamps of the world because these people were panty-waists." The part that makes me laugh most, though, is: "The British don't know how to make a good cup of coffee. You don't know how to make a good cup of tea. It's an even swap." In all fairness, the handbook is very helpful in outlining the weather, topography, language, and culture of England as well as encouraging friendly relations between the Americans and the British. Hitler and his propaganda chiefs try to create distrust between our two countries because, if he can do that, he has a greater chance of winning. The handbook helps bridge any gaps between our countries in an effort to unite us.

With the information they have learned from the handbook and twelve hour passes from the Army, soldiers can proceed to neighboring towns for leisure activities. The nearest city is Exeter which was bombed in '42 but has been cleaned up and repaired a bit. There are many shops in Exeter so it is a favorite place for GIs. In an area marked for demolition, called High Market, shopkeepers have set up stalls and are happy to have this new influx of customers. Children seem to think Americans are rich and they fraternize with the soldiers in a way that shows they are in awe of their clean uniforms and the chocolate they share. They laugh as the men ask them, "Do 'ya want some gum, chum?" I think it does the men good to make children smile, especially children who have already seen so much destruction from the war, their town practically flattened by bombings.

We also enjoy going to the town of Torquay. Here there are clubs run by the Red Cross specifically for soldiers. Coffee, food and dancing are always present as is an escape from the tension attached to our reason for being overseas. We have infused some of our culture into these clubs: jazz, R&B, the Blues, the jitterbug. I have heard that the British think the jitterbug is scandalous, and that many are not happy with us for introducing such a vulgar dance, but the girls in the clubs don't seem to complain.

There is a shortage of British men right now, and our American GIs are taking full advantage. This does not make the British men who are still in the towns terribly happy. They see the soldiers' fresh new uniforms, see them passing out candy and chewing gum, and see them flirting with the girls in town. They know that American soldiers are paid five times more than the British, so they view them as rich and conceited. They say American GIs are "overpaid, oversexed, and over here." However, overall, this sentiment is held by the minority, and I think Americans are well liked and appreciated.

The Red Cross not only opened clubs for soldiers but has also created what they call "Clubmobiles." These are London Greenline buses refurbished to be used as roaming donut and coffee stations. Volunteers drive the buses from place to place and make warm donuts and coffee for the troops. Soldiers enjoy this luxury as well as the conversations with the volunteers. It is a good morale boost. I understand there are plans for several of these mobile units to come ashore after we invade as well. I have a great deal of respect for the women who are willing to put themselves in harm's way in order to provide some relief to our men. (It makes me think of Bunny, and the endless hours she spent volunteering for the Red Cross during the last war. She is a wonderful wife, always such a support to me.)

Aside from pub hunting and dancing at clubs, we can go to the cinema on weekends. We have come to call this "canned morale." It is an escape for a few hours and it is a favorite pastime. In addition to a flick, we also go to watch the newsreels and cartoons. I imagine the people of the town are happy to see so many soldiers because just a few years ago, movie houses were closed (too risky with all the air raids).

We also have some fun back at camp too. The U.S.O. came once and their troupes sure know how to entertain! The performers had to sign an oath of secrecy upon arrival. "You are in the Army now," they were told. And we welcome them as part of our 4th Infantry Division if this is what they bring with them. The most popular songs were sung, jokes were told, and we were given a mammoth show.

For men who are, undoubtedly, feeling increasingly nervous about the upcoming invasion, finding a release is essential and entertainment in these cities, as well as from the U.S.O., is much appreciated. Staying busy both day and night helps us escape the full enormity of what is yet to come.

MAY 20, 1944
JOURNAL — TEDDY ROOSEVELT, JR.

I have been in a few wars now. I have been in different divisions and in different regiments. I have been everything from a young soldier to a Brigadier General. In every case, in every year of my service, I have been struck by the brotherhood that exists among men who fight together.

Life during deployment can be brutal. Close quarters, months of grueling terrain, feeling lost in foreign lands, missing home, sleepless nights, unbearable weather—sharing all of this develops a sort of tribal connection, not unlike the tribes I witnessed on my journeys to gather specimens for museums. Like those tribes, there is a "oneness" among divisions and loyalty is prized above most else. There grows an unyielding tie among comrades at war.

When I was transferred from the 1st Infantry Division, it was really difficult. I couldn't say goodbye the way I wanted; my voice choked and my heart hurt. I was not sure I would be able to find the closeness I experienced with my original division anywhere else. I was wrong. I have quickly formed friendships within the 4th Infantry Division that are just as deep, just as meaningful, just as enduring. Tubby was introduced to me when I needed an example of a general who is not only sound on military tactics, but also a real leader. (I have seen too many generals who were neither). Furthermore, I met Roddy who has come as close to being a brother to me as anyone can. The men of the entire 4th Infantry Division are family to me, in such a short period of time. This is how I know that brotherhood, in the army, is a gift that often comes out of a grave situation.

From destruction, aggression, fear, and loss, emerges unalterable bonds. Men who at home might never meet, let alone socialize, are now forever connected. The bonds help ease innate fears and pull us together to work as a whole, always fighting for the man next to us over ourselves. Our friendships are a force beyond the battlefields and, when the war ends, though happy to be going home, we are saddened to say farewell to the men with whom we have been literally and figuratively entrenched.

It is a profound experience. As we will be called to assemble for the invasion in the next few weeks, I am reflecting on this.

JIM

MAY 23, 1944

Dear Rose,

As a child who lost both parents, I learned to lean on my brother, to rely on him, to cherish him as my only living relative. That formed a very strong, intimate connection between us, and it might have been stronger than other brothers' connections because we faced deep sadness and loss together. There will never be anyone closer to me than he was, though I have experienced similar bonds during my time in the Army.

There is a power in the brotherly bonds formed by men who are at war together. Just like my relationship with Robert, my relationships with my fellow officers and with the soldiers are rooted in loyalty, shared ideals, and honor. The men of rank seem to understand me best and recognize what makes me the person I have become. They have spent the most time with me, have heard my stories, and have learned to appreciate my sarcasm (I think). I know, to the enlisted men, I seem direct and blunt, no nonsense and straight forward. Sometimes, this might come across as slightly intimidating, but once they get past my approach to the military aspects of my life, I think they realize I am good-natured and loyal, more laid back than they realized (except when I am in battle, of course). No matter the rank, I know the men know they can count on me to put myself at risk to keep them alive. I have not been able to control much in my life, but I can control my actions and I show my love for these men through those actions.

Perhaps this brotherhood is partly why I have made a career of the military: to forge bonds that help to fill the missing bond in my civilian life, the hole Robert left. The men of the 4th Infantry Division have become family to me after all these years, and I feel that even more as we head into the invasion together. Our loyalty to each other is a powerful connection that will keep us fighting, bravely. I cannot bear the thought of letting these men down. I would die for every one of these men, and they for me. As I wish I could have for Robert.

Steadfast and Loyal,
Uncle Jim

TEDDY

MAY 26, 1944
JOURNAL — TEDDY ROOSEVELT, JR

I have been asking Tubby to allow me to go with the assault companies, disembarking at H-hour with the first wave of troops, when we finally invade. He has been denying my requests. He told me it is against protocol for a general to go in with the first wave, that leading from the front, in this case, is not a wise move when the casualty rate is expected to be high. (I think he does not want to be responsible for the death of another of President Roosevelt's sons as well). He also kindly reminded me that I am much older than the average soldier being sent at H-hour, and that the beach will be difficult to maneuver (in other words, an old general who needs a cane just to walk on solid ground, will have a harder time on sandy terrain). Each time I have asked, he has repeated his reasons. He recently added that it would not be good for the morale of the troops to see me die, that everyone loves me and would be unable to advance in the event of my death. He is being realistic as his position requires, but I can argue my own merits on each point.

My proper place is in command of combat troops. It is why I repeatedly requested to be assigned to the European front. I know this invasion will be remembered for a long time and I want to be part of it. I want to aid in its success. I have the most experience of anyone with amphibious landings, already having experienced three amphibious landings with my previous division. I have led from the front many times (although criticized extensively for doing so). I know the officers assigned to the regiment that will be leading the first wave of troops and we work well together. I operate well under fire, I am observant and calm, and my leadership can help the men, many of whom have never seen a day of combat in their young lives.

The first wave determines the ultimate success of this invasion. If we do not break through the crust, the groups following us will not get in. Sending me in with the first wave allows me to receive accurate information, to have an overall picture for the incoming commanders, and to provide details in which they can place confidence.

We will be attacking the most heavily fortified coast in history. The Germans are well armed and ready for us. They will know we are coming because there will be no way to hide our movements in the harbors of southern England. I may be older, and walking with a cane, but it steadies the men to see me there with them. I know this is the way I can contribute the most.

All this I have outlined in a written request which I handed to Tubby today. I am not giving up. I will be in with the men at H-hour.

> May 26th 44.
>
> To Major General R.O. Barton C.G 4th Inf Div.
>
> 1) Since your informal refusal of my request to go in with the assault companies I have given much thought to the question and decided to request reconsideration because of the following facts.
> 2) The force & skill with which the first elements hit the beach & proceed may determine the ultimate success of the operation.
> 3) The rapid advance inland of the assault companies is vital to our effort as the removal of underwater obstacles cannot be accomplished unless the beach is free from small arms fire.
> 4) With troops engaged for the first time the behavior pattern of all is apt to be set by those first engaged.
> 5) Considered accurate information of the existing situation should be available for each succeeding element as it lands.
> 6) You should have when you get to shore an overall picture in which you can place confidence.
> 7) I believe I can contribute materially on all of the above by going with the assault companies. Furthermore I know personally both officers and men of these advance units and I believe that it will steady them to know I am with them.
>
> Theodore Roosevelt
> B.G. U.S.A

Teddy's formal, written request to join the first wave of troops on D–Day, this copy found among Uncle Jim's citations in his binder

JIM

MAY 30, 1944

Dear Rose,

Since being told that our division has been chosen to spearhead the upcoming invasion, our moods have been more sober. The tension is palpable as we end this month, knowing what is waiting for us in the next month, but our division is ready for what will be an invasion like no other in history's past. We are well armed, well trained, and well prepared. Most of the men here have been training since we were in the United States waiting to be called up. We have been training for manvy years now and every man is thoroughly familiar with his particular job.

Here, in England, we have been training in a center created for instruction, practice, and drills specific to our upcoming invasion. Residents were evacuated in a nearby town, Slapton Sands. Many of the townspeople, in all their lives, had never left Slapton Sands, but we needed to use that area in order to be well prepared. The terrain-containing a gravel beach, a strip of land, and a lake-was chosen because it resembles the area where we will land on D-Day. It is integral that we are accustomed to topography that is similar to where we will invade.

For months now, men have been trained in the use of assault weapons and in new skills required to advance when armored vehicles may not be able to provide support. Endurance tests, obstacle courses through sand and dunes, and even lessons in basic foreign phrases have been set up so that our actual landing will not feel as foreign to us. The area is also designed to mimic an enemy counterattack. There are concrete blocks to represent pillboxes, structures to imitate ship ramps, barbed wire, hedgehog exercises, and more. Regiments are led through drills under combat conditions much like the way we were when at Camp Gordon Johnston in Florida.

Training, since we arrived in England, moved into high gear and we have been rehearsing all aspects of the invasion simultaneously: embarkation drills, assault using live ammunition, twenty-five mile hikes to be completed in seven hours, practice with firearms (using dummy ammunition), camouflage, pole charges, really anything you can think of—the practice is meant to feel like the real thing. We even have air and naval battalions staged to resemble German opposition. General Eisenhower feels that the men need to be hardened by the experiences of real battle conditions and he wants to prepare the troops for the sights, the sounds, and even the smells of bombardment.

As we practice, we also recognize details that were not anticipated, details that need addressed before our actual invasion. Weak spots have been uncovered and discussed, removed or shifted. This gives us time to regroup and support the troops with additional training and tools as well. Some officers have even found themselves with new assignments along the way.

Up until today, speculation ran high concerning the ultimate destination of our invasion and the part the 4th Infantry Division would play in actual operations. No information had been divulged due to the necessity for strict security. Details were given only to a few men, and only those men knew the complete plan. All but a few were unaware of the extent of the operation until today.

Today, we were moved into marshalling areas and there is tight security; no one else is allowed to enter and no one is allowed to leave. The twelve hour passes to neighboring towns for evening activities abruptly stopped, and briefing of battalion staff, company commanders, and key personnel commenced just as abruptly. Soldiers were taken into tents in groups and shown sand tables that detail the invasion site to scale. They were shown a large topographical map and were told to memorize it. Soldiers turned in old equipment and were issued new equipment that had been held for last minute use. Troops lined up to turn in English money and, when this was returned in French currency, our ultimate destination was no longer a secret. Soldiers now know we are going to France!

The excitement surrounding the forthcoming mission has now increased to high pitch. Our division is ready. We will be the first to step foot in France from the sea and we will be an integral part of the invasion. We will be putting ourselves in a dangerous situation, walking straight into enemy fire, but we are prepared. There will be a lot of casualties, to be certain, but that is one of the harsh realities of war. We need to do what we came here to do — restore peace throughout Europe.

This will be the last of my letters for a while as mail home, including this one, will be curtailed and impounded for an undisclosed period of time. The hour of embarkation is imminent. I will write soon.

Steadfast and Loyal,
Uncle Jim

Uncle Jim's foreign currency (5 Franc note would have been with him on D-Day; 10 Franc note would have been with him around the Battle of the Bulge) found in his binder

JIM

JUNE 10, 1944

Dear Rose,

    I am hopeful this letter will reach you quickly so that you can tell the rest of our family that I am alive, well, and proud. A few days after my last letter, we were boarded on ships to leave England. An abrupt squall in the channel kicked up a heavy sea, so we were on the ship longer than expected, waiting in the harbor for better weather and low tides. We waited, not knowing when the time would come to move out, and when we got the word, the mood on the ship shifted, especially for the men who were to spearhead the invasion, the men who were chosen to be the first infantry on the beach. When we finally weighed anchor and headed out, we knew that this would alert the enemy, so we steamed ahead with periodic changes in direction to confuse the enemy.

    There was little sleep for the 8th Infantry Regiment on the night of June 5, into the early morning of June 6. It was like the night before a game. Each man lay in his bunk in the troop compartment or sat on the floor of the recreation room midship, chain smoking, talking to the man next to him, and anticipating what might befall him within the next twenty-four hours. There were mixed emotions of pride, sorrow, excitement, and fear. The fear was understandable, knowing they faced a grueling, bloody campaign, but their long, precise training gave them the courage they needed without any outwardly visible apprehension. In some ways it was a relief after many months of tedious training where the overall thought was to just finish this sordid business so they could get back to living their normal lives.

I was at the front of the ship, near the first wave of troops scheduled for H-Hour, watching as they readied to board landing crafts. Other men watched too, thinking ahead to their own embarkation, dreading the possibility of seeing a friend dead on the beach and on the route of advance inland. The mood became morose for these men. It might be the last time they would see their friends. For the first wave, though, there was not much opportunity for morbid reflection as they were given last minute instructions, a final drag on a cigarette, and a slap on the back before climbing aboard the crafts.

Ahead of our division, just before dawn, fleets of bombers bombed enemy installations on the beach and inland in order to eliminate enemies who threatened the advance of the assault units on board the landing crafts. Paratroopers landed behind German defenses with the mission of capturing the town beyond the beachhead and eliminating other enemy installations. Battleships began their barrage of fire on the enemy positions that were commanding beach strongpoints and the exits leading inland from the beach. Specially trained Navy personnel cleared underwater obstacles. Thus, the annihilation of the enemy coastal defenses began before our men left the landing crafts to storm the beaches.

The entire plan was smooth, coordinated, and magnificent, the climax of over two years of preparation. It was the greatest amphibious operation than had ever been attempted. But, most magnificent of all were the men in the assault crafts approaching the beach, their eyes focused on that narrow strip of sand, their rifles loaded and ready for immediate use, their bodies tensely anticipating the moment when the boats would stop and let them embark. Alongside them was Ted, who voluntarily assigned himself to the task of coordinating the initial attack at H-Hour.

Much to our surprise, the currents, the smoke from the advanced air and naval bombardment, a Navy guide boat that was sunk, and the overcast sky, landed the infantry 2,000 yards south of their target location. Ted had to think quickly and devise a new plan of attack. Even with the naval bombardment, there remained many enemy strongpoints due to their strong construction and deep placement, and Ted was near an active enemy defense. The enemy was delivering direct, observed artillery, machine gun, and small arms fire from a distance of 100 yards and over, and Ted was in the middle of it with his men. He was confronted by the reality that it would be hopeless to return defensive fire, so he made his way up the beach to closely observe the causeways and the remaining enemy emplacements. He returned to his men, contacted commanders, and coordinated an attack of the defenses that were barring the advance of the troops to the causeways. Ted and his men knocked out beach defenses and took German prisoners. When Col. Van Fleet arrived, he was surprised that the casualties were very light in comparison to anticipated numbers and equally impressed with the result of the initial landing.

The day just continued from there. The enemy possessed great fire power from all types of weapons, and they used that to their greatest advantage, but the defenses were not stubborn, and we cleared the beach. The prisoners we took were surprised that Allied troops were able to breach the defenses their leaders had declared to be impregnable. Our division had just under 200 casualties that morning, with 60 of those being an artillery battery that hit a mine. We achieved our initial objective and now we are continuing to advance towards our next.

Steadfast and Loyal,
Uncle Jim

8th Infantry Rgt. Is Cited as First To Land D-Day

FIRST ARMY HQ, Aug. 13—The Eighth Regiment of the Fourth Infantry Division made the first landings on the beaches of the Cotentin (Cherbourg) Peninsula, it was revealed yesterday in an official citation from the War Department.

"They stormed the prepared beach defenses," the citation read "and upon securing these cleared the causeways within their sector and drove inland, clearing the way for successive units by a continuous and courageous drive.

"This entire operation was carried out under heavy artillery fire and extensive sniping by small isolated groups in addition to regular enemy infantry troops in their path of advance.

"Upon landings of other units, the Eighth Infantry Regiment was moved into position on the left flank of the division. Their sector included a main communications line to the north which was strongly defended at successive positions.

"In the face of constant enemy artillery, rocket and small arms fire," the citation concluded, "they made a courageous and determined drive for three days and nights without letup."

Newspaper clipping, found in Uncle Jim's scrapbook

A G E N T

There was little sleep for men of the 8th Infantry on the night of June 5th and during the early morning of June 6th. It was like the night before the big game. Each man lay in his bunk in the troop compartment or sat on the floor of the recreation room amidship, chain smoking, talking to the man next to him, and anticipating what might befall him within the next twenty-four hours. The crews of the transport prepared hot breakfast for the assault parties which would leave the ships before dawn. A number of men not in the initial assault landings volunteered to assist in serving and preparing the meal. One of these men was particularly receptive to the mood of his comrades on D-day, and described it thus:

"I was on the USS Dickman with assault elements of the 1st Battalion and attached troops. I was more interested in the psychological reaction of the men with whom I had been intimately associated for two and one-half years, than in volunteering for a dirty job just to be a good guy. I dreaded the coming of H-hour as much as the men who'd hit the beach. I think that I was principally afraid that I might see some of my friends shot up on the beach and on the route of advance inland. As the men came through the chow line between two and three o'clock in the morning of the 6th, they were like high strung race horses, nervous, frightened, some morose. I knew as I spoke to each man that it might be for the last time. They were probably aware of it too, but were a hard determined looking group, resolved to do their job and oddly enough much less frightened, in much better emotional shape and much better steeled against the things they would see and go through, than many troops attached to us who had been through previous invasions. As the men sat down to eat, all apprehension seemed to vanish abruptly and was replaced by an almost festive mood of troops on maneuvers. After breakfast the men returned to their quarters, strapped on their equipment and awaited directions of the Dickman's loud speaker system to go to their assault boats. As each man finished breakfast and secured his equipment, he did not have long to wait before being called. There was not much time or opportunity for morbid reflection. Last minute words of instruction from his officer, a cigarette and a slap on the back with a word of God Speed from his Chaplain sent each 8th Infantryman into his boat with a feeling of self-confidence and assurance that the operation would be a great success."

Just prior to dawn, huge fleets of bombers flying across the channel from England, bombed vital and strategic enemy installations on the beach and inland which threatened the advance of the assault units toward their first objective. During the night American Paratroops of the 501st Parachute Regiment and Airborne Infantrymen of the 101st Airborne Division had landed behind German defenses in the vicinity of Ste Marie Du Mont with the mission of capturing the town, holding it until the arrival of the 8th Infantry, and in the meantime creating havoc among enemy troops and installations. Thus the annihilation of enemy coastal defenses had actually begun before the first ground troops hit the beach.

As the dawn wiped away the darkness, the beach became visible against the higher ground and wooded areas of the coast. The Air Force had commenced bombing the beach at H minus five hours and as the dawn became progressively

- 4 -

S E C R E T

Portion of 8th Regiment After Action Report, written by Uncle Jim, 4th Infantry Division, 8th Regiment Archives. (Notice much of this letter is taken verbatim from this report.)

SECRET

lighter, it was possible to distinguish orange flashes of the bomb bursts in relation to definite positions on the beach. At H minus forty minutes, the Battleships Nevada and Enterprise, with supporting heavy and light cruisers and destroyers, laid down a devastating barrage of fire on beach strong points and enemy positions commanding the beach and its exits to inland routes of advance. Until 0600 the assault boats which had been loaded with their personnel and equipment several hours previously, had circled their transports awaiting the moment for rendezvous on the basis of their respective assault waves. Approximately one-half hour before H-hour, the first assault waves of the 1st and 2nd Battalions rendezvoused and started toward the beach to predetermined points of landing which were then in the process of being cleared of under water obstacles by specially trained Navy Personnel. It was a marvelous picture; one that almost defies description. It is difficult to imagine the thousands of craft off the Cotentin Peninsula. It was the climax of moving about in the channel off the Cotentin Peninsula. It was the greatest amphibious operation which had over two years preparation. It was smooth, perfectly coordinated and magnificent, but, ever been attempted. It was smooth, perfectly coordinated and magnificent. the most magnificent thing about it was the men in the assault crafts approaching the beach, their eyes focused on that narrow strip of sand, their rifles loaded and ready for immediate use, their tense expectant bodies anxiously awaiting the moment when the boats would come in through the surf, permitting them to wade ashore, reduce the enemy strong points there and close with the soldiers of the Third Reich in hand to hand combat.

Heavy Naval fire continued to destroy enemy fortifications and pin down enemy on the beach until just before the landing by the assault troops. In order to effectively and completely explain the landing operation, we will turn for a moment to an account of unusual heroism before going on to further events of the establishment of the initial beach head.

At 0630, Brigadier General Theodore Roosevelt, Jr., landed on Utah Beach with the foremost assault elements of Company "E", 8th Infantry. General Roosevelt, Assistant Division Commander of the 4th Infantry Division, voluntarily assigned himself the task of coordinating the initial attack on the enemy beach strong points by the assault troops of the 8th Infantry at H-hour, on D-day, until the arrival of the Regimental Commander, Colonel James A. Van Fleet. The Navy landed the 1st and 2nd Battalions of the 8th Infantry, one thousand yards south of the previously designated point of debarkation. Immediately aware of the mistake upon landing, General Roosevelt, with complete disregard for his own life, went on a personal reconnaissance to determine the location of the causeways which had been designated as points of exodus for the troops from the beach proper. Although the Navy had previously laid down a heavy barrage which reduced many emplacements on and commanding the beach, many still remained in operation by virtue of deep, solid construction. At the time of General Roosevelt's reconnaissance, these fortifications and supporting positions, containing enemy machine guns and supporting riflemen, were delivering direct, observed artillery, machine gun and small arms fire upon the assault troops and upon him from a distance of one hundred yards and over. Confronted by the intensity and almost hopeless aspect of this defensive fire, General Roosevelt, personally made his way up the beach to a point where he could clearly observe the causeways, the approach to them, and the defensive fortifications which protected them and adjacent areas. He returned to the point of landing, and contacting the commanders of the 1st and 2nd Battalions.

- 5 -

SECRET

After Action Report, written by Uncle Jim, detailing Teddy's actions before VanFleet arrived

UNPACKING YESTERDAY | 77

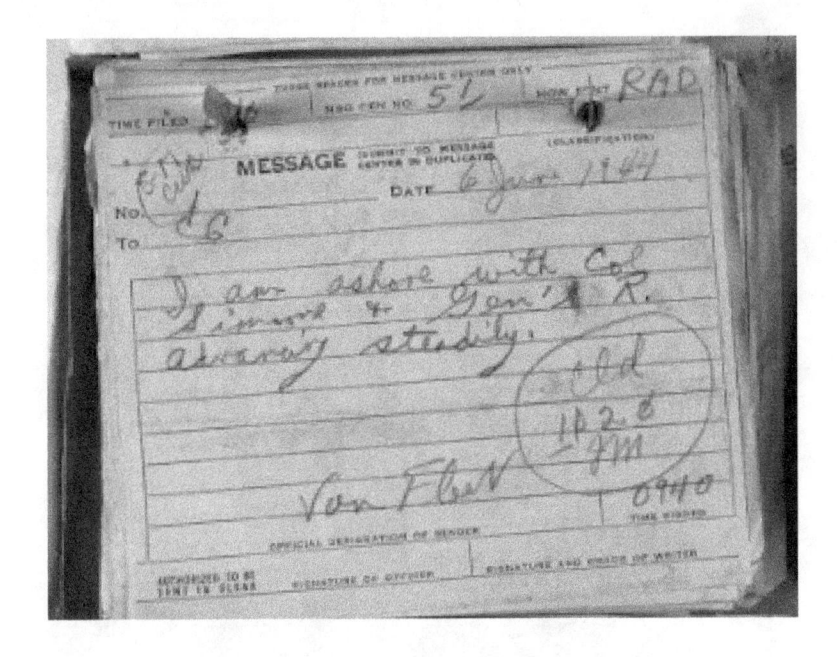

Signal Corps communication log — showing VanFleet's arrival at 9:30am on D-Day.

TEDDY

JUNE 10, 1944
JOURNAL ENTRY — TEDDY ROOSEVELT, JR

Now that I have time to sit down and internalize the start of the Normandy invasion, I want to make sure I put pen to paper and record my account of that day—June 6, 1944. What a day that was! What a day!

Several days prior, personal effects had been labeled, put in footlockers, and stored away in England. The men were now only identified by their dog-tags, their individuality melded into a unified group. We were loaded onto the large transport ships and waited for several days to move out because the weather would not cooperate. With strong winds and heavy rain, we had to button up and button down while stationary in the harbor, the ship becoming a sweatbox of nerves. No one knew the day or hour we would be told to load the smaller boats, and men avoided expressing their fears, though fear was palpable. Finally, after three days of waiting, we moved out. Then, on June 6, at 0130, we were told to move to our assembly stations. First, we were sent to blackened corridors to adjust our eyes to the darkness and then we boarded the transport boats which were ready to be lowered. I didn't use the ladder net to climb down, and men tried to help me drop the five feet or so from deck to boat, but I pushed them away with my cane. (I was not in need of assistance, and I would be leading them when we disembarked! They needed to see me as a soldier, not a hobbling, old man!)

Once loaded, the boats motored to the drop point for three hours. The men, previously eager to fight, now wondered if they were brave enough. We hunched over at the shoulders, our foreheads touching the back of the soldier to our front, in an attempt to stay dry, but it was to no avail. The salty sea spray drenched us and we were chilled to the bone. Wearing packs that must have weighed 70 pounds, the men were now wearing wet uniforms that increased the overall weight. In addition to their packs, they had life belts, gas masks and chemical weapon detectors, and toggle rope around their shoulders for crossing the flooded areas we expected to encounter behind the dunes.

Our uniforms, which were treated to repel gas in case of a chemical attack, were now drenched with sea water and smelled terrible. Men vomited. The stench, the cold air, the uniform smell, and the wetness was a revolting combination. As we got closer to the shore, the smell of oil from all the destroyers in front of us filled our lungs and more vomiting commenced. The men were tired, wet, cold, and scared out of their minds.

This was why I was there. This was why I wanted to be with the first wave of men. I had done this before. I knew what to expect and how to be successful. I knew that I would be able to steady the men and keep them moving forward, many of them so young, having never fought in any battle, let alone one this extreme. I talked with the men and calmed their nerves as the noise close to shore became overwhelming. Bombs being dropped by air support in advance of our landing, mines exploding, enemy artillery, waves pelting against our craft, and the engines from our landing crafts (now in line side-by-side) was deafening and terrifying at the same time.

Finally, our landing crafts lined up, twenty in a row. As each Higgins Boat got into fairly shallow water, the sailor driving the boat dropped the ramp and the men scrambled out into the unknown. The water was only waist high for most men (a little higher for a man of my height), but the water was full of ditches and holes that could turn that waist deep water into a sudden drop that put the water over even a tall soldier's head. Furthermore, the Germans knew we had arrived and there were bullets raining down around us. Stevie was sure we were both going to die. We had 200 yards of water to wade through until we could reach sand and we had no protection in the wide, open area. I saw several men go under, caught off guard and weighed down by their packs. Cries for help from men who were wounded or drowning now added to the maddening noises around us. I had to keep moving forward, blinders on.

When we finally stepped foot on the sand, I looked around and knew something was wrong. The red roofed house we had been trained to look for was not where it should be. There was a house on the seawall which should have been void of any structures. Surrounded by machine gun spray, the men moved to the closest place of perceived safety to regroup and organize. I had to think quickly. I sent a soldier to find the ruined windmill we had used as a marker during our strategy meetings and he discovered that it stood in a different location than it should have relative to our landing. Pulling all of these observations together, I realized we had landed south of our intended mark. The entire operation hinged on a swift advance that cleared the beaches for the rest of the troops landing after us. Additionally, if we did not clear our objective on schedule, we would not link up inland with the 82nd and 101st Airborne (who were dropped behind enemy lines six hours prior to our landing in order to take out enemy artillery and block reinforcements leading to the beach). Incoming waves of infantry were depending on us, the paratroopers were depending on us, and the people of France were depending on us! We had no choice but to carry-out the mission from an unplanned zone. So, I told the men close to me, "Well, we'll start the war from here!"

I was careful to notice the details of our new surroundings so I could relay them to future waves of men, while I pushed the men forward, plodding along with my cane, only armed with a 45-caliber pistol. (At some point I took shrapnel to my hand, which I consider a proud war wound.) Our men crossed the beach, clearing small arms fire, and began to move inland to kill or capture the enemy, crossing the flooded areas in order to meet the 82nd and 101st Airborne at the designated locations. As the troops continued on, I returned to the causeways to share details with incoming commanders.

I must have walked 20 miles that day, up and down the beach, swinging my cane to direct traffic while making sure there was no confusion over the sudden change in plans. I didn't want there to be chaos at the landing sites, for that would certainly invite German counterattacks!

Around 1030, I saw General Barton arrive on shore. He almost knocked me over with a bear hug, tears in his eyes. He had not expected to see me alive and he seemed overcome with joy to find me there, not only having survived the attack, but now providing valuable information. I have so much admiration for that general, I really do!

Bulldozer units moved up and down the beach to create paths through the dunes, push landing craft back to the sea, and assist vehicles as they became stuck in the sand. German artillery still constantly fired around us, but I was at my best. This is what I was born to do and it felt good. More and more waves of troops arrived and I met them with cheer. "Good day for hunting, men! Glad you could make it," I would shout and the men would laugh. As soldiers arrived to fight the enemy, it was my job to put them at ease.

For the rest of the day, I rallied the men, moving back and forth and showing them where to go, until the beach was secure and we were ready for the next phase. At that point, Stevie drove up with my jeep, a welcome sight after so much walking. I loaded my aching old bones into the jeep and we drove away, leaving a good day's work behind us.

JIM

JUNE 13, 1944

Dear Rose,

We have a division of men who are feeling rather slighted at the moment. We are receiving news from home that a lot of divisions are being credited with the Allied advances here in France, but there has not been any mention of the Ivy Division, our great 4th Infantry Division! How can this be? The 4th spearheaded the amphibious landing and had great success in crossing the so-called "impregnable seawall!" It was our division that landed first, at 0630 hours, H-Hour on D-Day! It was our division whose success enabled the success of all the units that came across the beach after us! Our entire 4th Infantry Division had come ashore by early afternoon—all three regiments of our division! Do you even know the significance of the speed and skill required to be able to do that?

I did not tell you in my last letter that I was on LST282 that day. The ship had only recently arrived from the United States and had only been in service for six months. The communications were in poor shape and we spent considerable time getting them into shape. I shared the command cabin with Commander Tomlinson, U.S. Navy, the commander of the flotilla. (He gave me some silver coins from France and told me that the war had caught him in France and that he would never have a chance to spend them.) We quickly followed the initial waves of troops to unload the armored tanks and vehicles needed for inland assault and supply transport. We had to fight weather that created strong currents and waves, making travel difficult. Another LST was torpedoed and sunk on its way and we were lucky it was not us. Smoke from the assault, strong currents, and wreckage from a destroyed ship caused a slight delay, but we overcame the confusion and made it to shore. When we were going ashore, one of my sergeants remarked, "Well if this was intended as a dry run, somebody sure got his signals crossed!"

By the end of the day, 1700 vehicles and 1800 tons of supplies were unloaded and ready for the next phase, ready to move inland before nightfall. To do this, the men before us had to destroy coastal forts — each containing massive, concrete blockhouses in a line, all with underground ammunition storage, interconnected trenches, and automatic weapon fortifications. There were also concrete sniper pillboxes to overcome, beach fortifications extending all the way up the coast, minefields, giant metal jacks called "hedgehogs" along the beach, and traps everywhere. All of these obstacles had to be eliminated or averted. The Germans had four years to prepare for this day and we still destroyed them in one day!

Why are the papers not detailing our part in this great invasion? Of the five beaches to be hit on June 6, Utah Beach was the first, and we spearheaded this invasion. I know June 6, 1944 will go down in history, and many of us are unhappy to hear that we are not even part of the narrative! You should be proud of our Ivy Division — we saw a lot of action, kept the casualty numbers low, met the 82nd and 101st Airborne inland, and helped push the enemy out of the towns just beyond the beach. All of this had to be well coordinated to be successful, and even with some mishaps, it was! While those who landed at Omaha Beach suffered more casualties than we did at Utah Beach, that does not mean we deserve minimal coverage in the press.

Steadfast and Loyal,
Uncle Jim

How Fourth Infantry Fought Through to Reach Paratroops

By Charles F. Kiley
Stars and Stripes Staff Writer

WITH THE FOURTH INFANTRY, France, June 17 (delayed)—The hard-fighting soldiers of the Fourth Infantry were brassed off today. After nine days and nights of bitter warfare without rest, from the Normandy beachhead to beyond Montebourg and on the road to Cherbourg, the boys of the "Ivy Division" heard that a lot of people were getting credit for the Allied advances in France. That is, almost everybody but the Fourth.

This is to let them know they were not entirely forgotten. The dead they left behind—enemy dead as well as their own—told a vivid story of their tireless efforts. Now that Supreme Headquarters has announced the presence of the Fourth in Normandy the world outside France also will be hearing the story.

The Fourth arrived on D-Day with the assault forces, fought its way under, through and over some of the toughest obstacles in the Cherbourg peninsula until it completed its primary mission. Not once did the Ivy Boys stop until this first job was done. Now they have a little time to lick their wounds and get a breather.

One regiment of the Fourth hit the beaches at H-Hour on D-Day with the other two following an hour or so later. Theirs was the unenviable mission of scrambling through the marshland flooded by the Jerries before the enemy backed up from the coastal zone on the west side of the peninsula. The third battalion of another regiment, commanded by Lt. Col. Arthur S. Teague, had to advance four miles through these inundated areas, most of the time up to their hips in mud and water. They made such rapid progress against these odds that some of the units closed with retreating Germans to engage them in hand-to-hand combat.

When the Fourth consolidated its units, it tossed regulation tactics into the Channel. Normally, a division moves with two regiments abreast, with a third in support. In order to move swiftly and according to schedule, the division put all three regiments abreast and started the struggle that made them fight uphill all the way.

Paratroopers had been in Ste. Mere Eglise one and a half hours after they dropped from sky transports, and the Fourth had to reach them in a hurry so as not to leave them stranded behind enemy lines without communications.

The Ivy Boys got through to the paratroopers after fighting past numerous strongly-fortified positions all along the coastal strip from the landing point to Ste. Mere Eglise.

The Jerries' 88s raised hell with the Ivy Boys as they moved, but for every man who fell hundreds kept the drive in high gear.

Gen. Taylor's Letter Salutes Famous 4th

Here's another tribute to the Famous Fourth and another reason why men of the division wear that Ivy Leaf patch proudly. It's an excerpt from a letter written to Maj. Gen. Harold W. Blakeley, the 4th's commander, by Maj. Gen. Maxwell D. Taylor, who parachuted into Normandy before dawn on D-Day as CG of the 101st Airborne Division. Wrote Gen. Taylor:

"I never fail to get a glow from the sight of the Fourth Division shoulder patch. I remember how good it looked to me on the morning of June 6, 1944."

Newspaper clippings found in scrapbook, detailing the 4th Division's involvement on D Day, in response to the news that no credit had been given to the Ivy Division

JUNE 14, 1944

Dear Rose,

Everyone has been telling stories about the initial landing that began this Normandy invasion. There are countless tales of bravery and sacrifice. Every story I hear fills me with such pride, knowing I am part of the greatest country on Earth, a country that has entered the European campaign to correct the wrong doings of evil men and to free the innocent people of their oppression. My favorite stories involve our division, of course, but there are a few stories involving civilians that I love just as much.

There is a large group of people here who are part of an underground movement that played a big role in the success of our invasion. They were willing to risk their lives for their part in the invasion because they have a desperate desire to be free of the enemy's occupation. They knew if they were caught it meant certain death, but it was a chance to help liberate their country, and, to many, death was not all that dissimilar to the life they were living under German rule.

Leading up to June 6, the people in resistance networks made secret contact with Allied commanders. They collected information that helped us know more about the enemy's position, strength, equipment, and plans. They gave descriptions of the local terrain which helped us prepare and train for the landings. They even discovered which specific German divisions were in the Normandy region, which gave us insight regarding the battle experience of the enemy guarding the area.

We communicated in coded messages over a London radio station. Although radios were confiscated by the Germans, there were plenty of people in France who listened on wireless sets, secretly. They then would relay the information received from coded messages and carry out missions accordingly. We also sent 16,000 homing pigeons into France and trained them to fly between England and France (They carried back messages written on rolled paper that was tied to their feet). And we sent paratroopers into France to supply French resistance with supplies and weapons.

Beyond intelligence operations, people in France also carried out sabotage missions. Weeks before our invasion, railroads were damaged, locomotives were derailed, all but one of the trains in Northern France were destroyed, and most of the bridges crossing the Seine River were blown up in coordination with Allied bombings. This ensured that German reinforcements could not be moved to the front.

The French Resistance prepared by training to use specific weapons. They carried messages through underground networks. There was even a group, a few years ago, who put sugar into cement mixers so that German bunkers were constructed with cement that was less strong.

On June 5, the night before our landing, coded messages were sent to let Resistance operatives know that our invasion was imminent and that sabotage missions, with maximum effort, should commence. We parachuted three-men special force teams (consisting of British, American, and French soldiers) into France to align Allied force missions with Resistance missions. Together, they disabled communication and power networks in the invasion area to prevent a concentration of German troops. Within hours of H-hour, in the areas closest to the beaches, they carried out sabotage missions in order to help secure our landing. Communication networks in the immediate vicinity were cut, which forced the Germans to use radio communication that could be intercepted, helping us know of their plans before, during, and after our initial invasion.

Finally, after our landing, French Resistance members continued to risk their lives even after our troops were engaged in the war. They served as guides to our troops because they had knowledge of the area, the terrain, and location of German positions. Many were killed, but just as our soldiers sacrificed so others could be free, the people in the Resistance were also willing to risk death for their own freedom. They even continued to help by rescuing Allied airmen who had been shot down, bringing them to first aid stations along the beach.

While I was near one of those first aid stations on the day we came to France, I encountered a French citizen, not from the Resistance network, but simply an ordinary citizen whose story made me even more aware of how important our contributions to this war truly are. This man and his family live on a dairy farm nearby and their home and farm had been taken over by the Germans for the past four years. They were forced to remain on their farm in order to provide milk for their oppressors. (It is hard to imagine the enemy taking over your home, living in your quarters, sleeping in your beds, and then forcing you to toil and provide for their comfort and wellbeing, isn't it?) Well, as we landed in France, the family was hiding in an outbuilding on their farm because they were afraid of how the Germans were acting, not realizing exactly what was starting to happen as we came ashore that morning. While in hiding, the family began to hear the sounds of a battle that was taking place in the adjoining cow field on their land. They were terrified so they stayed hidden until the noise subsided. When they felt safe to come out of hiding, the family's 23-year old son approached the small group of American soldiers who were leaving the field, holding a white handkerchief to show he and his family were friendly.

The son approached the soldiers with an anxious look on his face because he was seeing the carnage of the battle and trying to understand what had just occurred, what had been happening while he and his family had been hiding in an outbuilding. This anxious look and the fact that an unknown man was approaching the troops caused one soldier to be on alert. He did not see the man's white handkerchief, thought he was the enemy, and shot him five times with the intent to kill. The rest of the French family rushed with their hands in the air and explained the confusion, but the damage had been done. The son lay on the ground, seriously wounded.

He was rushed to the first aid station on the beach, where I encountered him, and where medics tended to him. As I was being told his story, he was quickly evacuated to England. Fortunately, doctors in England operated to save his life and he is now recovering, but he has a long road ahead of him. The story does not end there, though, and this is the part of the story that I really want to share with you. Incredibly, that man has told doctors that he not only forgives the American soldier who shot him, but is grateful to the Americans for his family's freedom. Isn't that extraordinary? An unarmed civilian, mistaken as the enemy and shot five times by his liberators, is grateful for what we accomplished on June 6. Though severely wounded at the hands of an American, he is finally able to say that the last four years of German occupation have come to an end and that evokes feelings of gratitude rather than mistrust or anger.

That is very significant to me. This shows that the work we are doing here is important and powerful, and that the people of France are kind, forgiving people. People back home may be hearing about the war from the perspective of our trained forces, but you should also know about the people in France who have been living under unfathomable conditions for the past four years. Every time we encounter a citizen of France, we are reminded of our reasons for being here, and we are proud to be fighting for their liberation. I feel that we will be forever connected, in these moments and on this day, historically and emotionally. So many brave people, both in France and on the Allied side, have risked their lives, and continue to risk their lives, in order to stop evil.

Steadfast and Loyal,
Uncle Jim

TEDDY

JUNE 15, 1944
JOURNAL — TEDDY ROOSEVELT, JR.

Today Roddy and I recalled our first experiences in the little town of St. Marie du Mont, which is the first town we entered after crossing the beach, located inland from the landing site. On D-Day, Stevie and I entered that town after leaving the causeways at day's end. The first thing I saw, quite poetically really, was the town's church. It is the centerpiece of the village, fixed proudly in the middle of the small town square, a mighty bell tower overlooking its citizens. I was struck by this glorious place of worship whose artillery damaged tower must have a view clear to the beach.

    I asked Stevie to stop the jeep and I got out to look around. When I went inside the church, clean-up was underway and there was a lot of dust. I noticed a pool of blood on the floor, and it felt like the mark of evil in a house of God; I was glad it would be washed away soon. Then, when I looked up, there was a large stained-glass window which was made up of many smaller panes, coming together to form the larger whole. It made me think of our division's three regiments — the 8th, 12th, and 22nd — pieces of a whole, separately melding together to form the larger 4th Infantry Division. I was filled with pride.

    Standing in this church, I was reminded of one of the scenes I saw on the beach that day, the day we began this Normandy invasion. Chaplain

Ellenberg, the Episcopal Chaplain of the 8th Regiment, had landed with the assault elements of the 2nd Battalion and he was an inspiration to behold. He worried only of his duties as a Godly man, no regard for his personal safety. On the beachhead, he moved among the wounded and dying, seemingly oblivious to the enemy artillery, machine gun, and small arms fire surrounding him. I later saw him at the Naval aid station on the beach, tending to the men. The station was under heavy artillery fire and all personnel were forced to take cover to protect themselves from shell fragments. The wounded and dying were left unprotected, on stretchers, unable to take cover themselves. Chaplain Ellenberg chose to remain exposed to the dangers and remained with the men who could not protect themselves. He stayed on his knees beside the wounded, praying with them while shells burst all around. So many fragments were spraying that his shirt was practically torn from his back, the cloth laying in rags against his body. He never stopped praying. On that day, 14 men were killed and 63 were wounded in his regiment. Chaplain Ellenberg sacrificed his life to provide comfort to these men. Many of the 14 who perished saw his comforting face as they passed, rather than being left alone to witness the horrors of war.

I thought of Chaplain Ellenberg as I stood in St. Marie du Mont's church. I looked at the light coming through the stained-glass window. I felt very emotional as I watched the men of God in this church sweeping away the signs of enemy occupation. It was a magnificent juxtaposition of elements. Good had triumphed over evil.

Chaplain Ellenberg, on the beach, knelt undisturbed as battle raged around him, a source of quiet for the men over whom he prayed. Similarly, while tanks and army transports were being ushered in and directed through the streets of St. Marie du Mont, standing still in the center of it all, was this magnificent church and its beautiful window of unity. Both the sight of Chaplain Ellenberg and the emotions I felt in that church, seemed to show us that peace may not be far away.

UNPACKING YESTERDAY | 93

Church in St. Marie du Mont, 1944 Army Signal Corps photo

JIM

JUNE 16, 1944

Dear Rose,

Looking back on our initial invasion on June 6, I am remembering my experience when I entered the small village just beyond the Atlantic seawall, St. Marie du Mont. As I watched the townspeople mingling with the soldiers and I looked around the town, it occurred to me that this place had already experienced so much physical and emotional destruction from the war, and so much loss.

A monument stood in the center of the town in remembrance of the townspeople who sacrificed during the last world war, and I noticed the surname "de Vallavieille" repeated—different men from the same family. They have experienced two wars now, twenty years apart. How many families in St. Marie du Mont were forced to mourn the deaths of loved ones lost in this war, already having done so during the last?

Thinking of the most recent conflict, I felt so much sorrow for the people here. Until this moment, for the past four years, the enemy had occupied their town, had stormed into their homes to claim as their barracks, had stolen their livelihoods, and had taken away their freedoms. The Germans had intimidated, oppressed, and even executed the people of this town, for four long years!

What will it be like for them, now, to return to the sights and sounds they knew before the war, before our invasion freed them of the enemy's tyranny? Would they be able to rebuild their lives and move past the horrors they endured? Would their homes feel the same, emotionally, as they reclaimed them, physically? Would they be able to feel safe, happy, and optimistic for the future? I hope they can return to a simpler time, to what their lives were like before the war, but I am not sure that will be possible. There is damage done to a person's spirit in times of war, in whatever way the war is experienced. The people of this town will have a hard time healing from this, surrounded by visual and emotional reminders of what they endured. Beauty has been tarnished by the beast.

Steadfast and Loyal,
Uncle Jim

Beth Rieman is in Mentor, Ohio
August 7, 2018 at 12:00 pm • Mentor, OH

My parents and I spent the week at home going through several boxes of my grandmother's belongings, unopened for the past 15+ years. Along the way, we found some pretty incredible things and learned so much about my grandmother's family, things we didn't know as deeply as we do now. (I swear I cried three times a day as we unboxed new treasures!)

One discovery, last night, was beyond incredible. Remarkable, actually. The kind of discovery that gives you goosebumps and leaves you shaking from the adrenalin rush. When we realized what we had, we sat in awe. We researched and compared pictures and checked off the boxes until we knew what we had was real.

When I came home today to tell the story to my family (a story I rehearsed in my head the entire drive), I could not finish without crying. I just feel that it is so important to leave a legacy and, for one relative who has no family left, we are going to be able to do that for him.

Last night/this morning, at 2:00 am, I sent an email outlining what we discovered to the right people and we are now in touch with a specific museum to donate a memorable, and in our opinion, significant, piece of WWII history. I know the process may take a while, but I am excited to see how the rest unfolds, excited to donate this item to a place that makes sense as a final resting place. In this way, the legacy is shared with so many.

More to come when I can figure out a way to put this in words and share it here...

TEDDY

JUNE 17, 1944
JOURNAL — TEDDY ROOSEVELT, JR.

This Normandy invasion was supposed to encompass two weeks, but we are behind schedule as we try to overcome the difficult topography of this area and the stiff German resistance. In order to make a break-through on the sector south of Carenton, we have to clear the rugged terrain. The terrain is full of swampy rivers and marshes, and vast networks of interlocking hedgerows that have orchards within their perimeters. It is impossible to see into the areas beyond the hedgerows and from one field to the next. In this small area of Normandy, there are thousands of these fields!

These areas prove ideal for German defensive positions, but difficult for Allied offensive positions. Narrow, sunken roads are the only paths between 15-foot tall hedges, so we cannot get tanks through the area and we are easily ambushed as well. Yet, we have to reach firm ground on which we can use armored equipment, which means we have to fight the enemy and try to clear the way at the same time. The 4th Infantry Division has been assigned this task.

"Task" sounds like we have been given a chore, a job to complete in order to earn an allowance. That is far from the reality of this style of fighting and the battles we have in the hedgerows are grim. Germans are permanently entrenched in every hedgerow, dug in every few yards. The hedgerows are lined with dugouts, covered foxholes, and weapon emplacements that are hard to locate even at close range. The Germans have the advantage. They can stay put, while we have to move ahead to accomplish our "task." Their positions also give them the advantage of protection as the hedges keep them blocked from overhead fire. They have trained for nearly four years to fight in this terrain and they made sure to keep hedgerows intact when they were flooding the peninsula so they would have many advantages when we invaded.

Moving forward among orchards, hedgerows, and swampy areas is not easy. A 100-yard gain is a full day's work. We cannot fully gain a picture of the area since our views are blocked and we cannot easily maneuver either. Every forward movement is met with enemy fire from places we cannot see, places hidden within the hedgerows. An assault spanning the course of days clears out an area no larger than a backyard garden because the hedges' root systems are so deeply locked together that even strong machinery cannot wipe them out. We cannot run them over with tanks because that exposes the underbelly of precious machinery and gives Germans an easy target to destroy. We have used explosives to blow holes in the hedges in order to bring tanks through, but that only attracts counterattacks. Following the explosions, bulldozers are needed to clear wider spaces, which just makes us more conspicuous as well. All of this helps the enemy to delay our advance. It is all very hard on the soldiers who are given this assignment, who really are only able to fight with rifles when having to move this way. Always, after a day of fighting, there is a frustrated weariness. There are times you might rather be exposed and take a hit than have to get back up and do it all over again.

I have been told that the army has men working to create attachments for tanks that will modify our armored divisions and allow them to break through hedgerows, but until that time, we are fighting the only way we know how: on our bellies, inch by inch.

JIM

JUNE 28, 1944

Dear Rose,

The town of Cherbourg has finally been captured and was liberated on June 25. Cherbourg was always deemed a necessary capture, a critical point. We needed to secure this deep-water port to allow reinforcements and supplies to be brought directly from the U.S. and to widen the area the Germans had narrowed in their purposeful flooding of the peninsula. This was a primary objective of the Normandy invasion, but it was not an easy fight.

We had to push through a broad front while destroying German headquarters, defenses, and forts from surrounding cities before we could even begin an assault on Cherbourg. We held the line at Montebourg and experienced a barrage so close it almost burned our faces. This kind of fighting was severe after many weeks of hedgerow fighting where our men had to crawl on their bellies from one hedgerow to the next, under direct fire.

As we moved through towns and villages, streets reduced to rubble, the townspeople would come out from hiding. I was struck by their appearance and wondered if we looked as ravaged as they. Their clothing was tattered and dirty, their eyes sunken. The people are tired and, I think, had begun to lose hope. When they saw us, though, they brought us glasses of water and smiles. They had hope again and they were very appreciative.

When we got closer to Cherbourg, we knew that we would face a difficult battle. The port city is surrounded by a ring of hills which Germans spent years fortifying before our arrival. Behind this, there were ancient French forts now occupied by Germans and these were surrounded by defenses. All of this was protected by minefields, barbed-wire, anti-tank ditches, and more. There were even underground trenches connecting fortifications. The Germans were going to stay and fight or fall where they stood, and we had to pull from our energy reserves to push hard against them.

The enemy defended the high ground of the city and shelled our entire regiment and lines of supply with heavy, effective fire. We used flame-throwers and had cannon support and bangalore torpedoes. The entire advance was bloody, with a lot of casualties on both sides, but we kept pushing forward, knowing Cherbourg was an essential capture.

One hero in this battle who stood out to me was Lt. John C. Rebarcheck. He was the only surviving officer of his company toward the end. In the last phases of battle, on the verge of complete physical exhaustion, nerves among his men were jumpy, tempers raw. Germans were firing every gun and fieldpiece directly at their group. And, somehow Rebarchek led his men against virtually impossible odds. He led them through a maze of tunnels, dugouts, and gun emplacements which boasted an amazing amount of fire power. Once within 150 yards of the strongpoint, Rebarcheck's company was pinned down by enemy fire and had to withdraw. So, when supporting tanks moved forward, under constant barrage of fire, Rebarcheck mounted a tank and stood calmly by its turret to lead his 51 remaining men towards the enemy. They engaged in hand-to-hand combat, Rebarcheck fighting among them with his rifle and bayonet, and the group successfully drove the enemy from its position. This left an indelible impression on all of us.

Another act of bravery that inspired us all was Ted's leadership. Ted led a reconnaissance group on foot, almost to the sea, in the final hours of the siege. He walked through areas infested by Germans, past strong points, past machine guns, past snipers-he led men half his age, walking ahead of the battalion, all the way!

There were many other examples of heroism, some recognized, some lost amidst the smoke and confusion of battle, but those were two that needed to be mentioned. Together, our heroic 4th Infantry Division and the 9th and 79th Infantry Divisions, along with support attacks from air and naval bombardment, met our target and liberated the city of Cherbourg. We fought hard for four days in the city and pushed relentlessly until we had won. We mopped up the remaining resistance for two more days and accomplished our objective. We are now, more than ever, determined to hurl the German Army back through Central France and decisively defeat it on its own soil.

As always, you must know that I draw strength from the memory of your father's courage and your grandfather's determination each day as I move towards another objective.

Steadfast and Loyal,
Uncle Jim

In Triple Squeeze On Cherbourg,
Vet, Green Yanks Victors

CHERBOURG, June 29.—(Delayed)—(INS)—Three U. S. divisions—two of them green, unproven troops and the other a veteran outfit from the North African and Sicilian campaigns—applied the triple-phased "squeeze" which led to Cherbourg's capture.

The French port's fall was effected by co-operation of the American Fourth, Ninth and 79th divisions. Of these, only the Ninth had previous battle experience, having been in on the kill at Bizerte, and Randazzo, Sicily. The Ninth fought also in the battle of Troina, Sicily.

Under command of Maj. Gen. Manton S. Eddy of Chicago, the Ninth division was brought into France some days after D-day in first-class fighting shape, and anxious to again prove its right to laurels won in previous campaigns in which military security deprived it of public recognition.

The Ninth was all set and, once turned loose, fought its way quickly across the peninsula. Then it swung northward, without encountering much opposition until in Cherbourg's outer line of defenses. Infantry assaults against the enemy's concrete strongpoints, in bitter hand-to-hand combat similar to that experienced by the other two divisions in the final five days of the battle, then began.

Earlier, one regiment of the Ninth had taken Quinville, storming strongpoint after strongpoint in conjunction with one regiment of the Fourth division.

The Ninth fought its way into Cherbourg from the southwest. The division already had plenty of experience in capturing cities. More-

SUPREME HEADQUARTERS, ALLIED EXPEDITIONARY FORCE, June 29.—(AP)—Maj. Gens. Charles Hunter Gerhardt and Clarence R. Huebner, both veterans of the last war, were revealed today as the commanders of two American infantry divisions in action in Normandy.

Gerhardt, U. S. graduate of West Point, is commanding the 29th infantry division. Huebner, who rose through the ranks from private after turning down a West Point appointment, commands the First.

Huebner, 55, fought in "the fighting first," in the last war when it was the first division to land in France.

Gerhardt's father was Brig. Gen. Charles Gerhardt, a graduate of West Point in 1887.

over, it had fought under Eddy in the battles of El Guettar and Sedjenane.

The Fourth division underwent its baptism of fire on the beach at the Grand Dune de Vereville on June 6, it being chosen by General Eisenhower and specially trained for the task of assaulting Hitler's Atlantic wall.

Under Maj. Gen. Raymond O. Barton of Ada, Okla., the Fourth never once failed to see a single day since D-day that at least one of its regiments was not advancing to take new ground. Main weight of its assault was carried from the beach, straight northwest to Cherbourg, engaging elements of five German divisions en route.

The Fourth still was going strong at the finish, knocking out numerous German positions ahead of schedule at such a rate that its original boundary was changed and it was permitted to enter Cherbourg simultaneously with other divisions capturing the southeastern part of the city.

Friendly rivalry between the American outfits was carried to such an extent that the 79th was hard put to keep the Fourth division out of its central sector.

As lieutenant colonel of the Eighth infantry regiment, Barton lowered the last American flag to fly over Germany on February 7, 1923, at the fortress at Ehrenbrinstein. Barton, nicknamed "Tubby," was born in Oklahoma Indian territory in 1899.

The 79th, under Maj. Gen. Ira "Bill" Wyche drove through the center of the peninsula into Cherbourg. Among the strong-points it encountered was Fort du Roule. It also engaged in bitter street fighting within the city.

Wyche, like Eddy, is strictly a front-line general and has had numerous narrow escapes. In the final days of the campaign, for example, he was trapped in a "screaming meemie" barrage and his jeep was pierced by shrapnel.

The army also released the names of Maj. Gen. Matthew Ridgeway, veteran commander of the 82nd airborne division, and Brig. Gen. Maxwell Taylor, commander of the 101st air-borne—both of whom parachuted into France before H-hour of D-day.

Ridgeway looks like any of his competent parachute officers—slim, compact, aggressive. T____ is the man who made a secret mission into Rome the day before Italy's surrender.

Newspaper clipping from Uncle Jim's scrapbook, discussing Cherbourg's capture

TEDDY

JUNE 28, 1944
JOURNAL — TEDDY ROOSEVELT, JR.

After the capture of Cherbourg, we had a ceremony in the city. Several hundred American soldiers stood on the streets and balconies around the town square and a few civilians stood as well. The buildings surrounding the square were shuttered and abandoned and the buildings around the harbor beyond were utterly wrecked. The town's statue of Napoleon was still surrounded by German barbed-wire. Everything showed signs of a city that had been under siege, a brutal fight for its freedom.

On the steps of the ravaged Hotel de Ville, General Collins read a speech in French while an honor guard made up of a platoon member from the 4th, 9th, and 79th Infantry Divisions, as well as three division commanders, stood by. The mayor of Cherbourg accepted a French flag made of American parachutes (the blue was a bit more on the green side, but the sentiment of the gesture was not lost). A band played and a few people danced. Then, the crowd slowly drifted away. This was not a huge celebration for the townspeople, as there aren't many civilians left in the almost completely empty town, but it was important to show the people of the city that they are finally free.

I have been appointed Military Governor of Cherbourg. My duties include restoring order and cleaning the great port so that it is ready to receive reinforcements. Many of the streets of Cherbourg are not recognizable, complete piles of rubble and debris. Many of the buildings have been destroyed and the wreckage also covers the streets. Bulldozers are needed to clear the rubble and the navy is working to clear the water of wreckage. The Germans intentionally destroyed the port prior to their surrender so the Army and Navy are working to make a temporary port at Utah Beach while we work to make this port operational.

The weather does not provide relief and my clothing is in a constant state of discomfort—wet and cold, clinging to my body. The men are exhausted from non-stop fighting, from a long drive against the German lines, from having faced heavy resistance. I will keep pushing myself to fulfill my responsibilities, but the task ahead is daunting. I must keep my energy levels high and my sense of humor engaged if I am to keep the soldiers' morale elevated.

JUNE 30, 1944
JOURNAL — TEDDY ROOSEVELT, JR.

As I watched Roddy walk away from HQ this evening, jabbing a soldier in the side, obviously having just delivered some good-natured teasing, I was struck by how different he is from what men expect when they first meet. I think most soldiers feel a little intimidated by Roddy with their first introduction to him. He is hard-working and diligent, and he gets a sort of focused determination at times that makes him come across as having an unapproachable demeanor, but that is only because of the weight of his responsibilities. His focus is intense on the work at hand, and the work is serious business—life or death business. Immediately, once he is pulled away from whatever he is completely focused on, the aloofness fades away and you notice him to be only good-natured and kind. One quickly realizes that he was only withdrawn, or seemingly unapproachable, because he was busy with important duties.

Roddy has a smile that changes the shape of his face. When he smiles, everything moves, every muscle, every hair, every inch of his face. It is like his whole face has come to life with the flip of a switch and the light really could fill a room. You are immediately drawn to his warmth and kindness. This kindness, though, is balanced with a sharp wit, and a sarcastic tongue. I am not sure I have ever met anyone who is as quick with playful jabs, as fast on their feet with funny comments inserted at just the right time. His personality is not so large as to be the center of attention, but rather a subtle banter that can leave an entire group rolling with laughter. He gets a playful grin on his face when he sees the reactions his humorous commentaries receive and then he quietly owns the room. He would have made a good senator with how he is able to draw people to him. Truly, if he were not a career military man, politics would have suited him well.

The leaders in the 4th Infantry Division have a great respect for Roddy. He knows many by name and makes it a point to do so. He always remembers specific details about a person's interests, life back home, and specific contributions on the battlefield. He asks questions and genuinely wants to know each man, not as a colonel, but as his brother in arms. Even his after action reports detail the human side of the war as if he is wanting to leave a permanent account of his men's actions in this war. The men look to him for advice and sometimes seek permission from him, but not out of fear, rather, because they trust him and they know that he would never ask them to do anything he wouldn't be doing right beside them. In fact, I have seen him put the risk solely on his own shoulders while telling his men to stand down.

Tubby Barton depends on Roddy, like a right-hand man. The two have a sort of unspoken language of their own. I have watched Tubby look Roddy's way and watched Roddy look back without saying a word.

This is then followed by a change in the look on Tubby's face to reveal another expression that only Roddy can understand. Entire decisions can be made this way, with just the expressions between them. To the same extent, they will finish each other's verbal thoughts and shorten conversations, the need for full sentences unnecessary when speaking their language. The rest of us will sometimes laugh because we have not understood any of the exchanges, niether the verbal or the unvoiced, but within a series of facial gestures and half sentences, decisions will be made and meetings will move forward. God bless anyone having to take accurate notes of any of the sessions!

Tubby depends on Roddy, the men respect him, and even the mess cooks are drawn to him. One of the cooks, Joe, told me that Roddy secretly brought snacks from the officers' quarters while they were on the boat to England (apparently Joe did not particularly enjoy the English fare he was ordered to prepare). Roddy reads people well and takes care of everyone, silently like he did with the snacks or overtly when he notices something is not sitting right with someone. I have often observed him asking to walk with a soldier, slowly removing from the group, because something has registered on his mental radar. I will then see them strolling, Roddy completely engaged in what is being said, listening intently, sometimes placing an arm across the soldier's back in a comforting gesture.

When dealing with the colonels commanding our regiments, Roddy becomes a little more gruff. His focus is on "killing the sonsabitches" and keeping his men safe. He resumes the determined focus he has with any task and becomes more serious. He follows protocol and delivers orders firmly because he knows war is a serious business (very similar to Tubby's demeanor). He rallies his men before an engagement and risks his life to rally them at the frontlines during battle. He pushes them because he knows their capabilities and knows it is important to keep their morale strong. His courage under fire is contagious and his men always meet their objectives, often by doing more than is expected.

Roddy really is a fine soldier, a caring brother, and my best friend here with the 4th Infantry Division. I am lucky to have the connection I have to him. It makes all of the terrible conditions in battle, all the miserable weather, and the terrible coffee here, much more bearable.

James S. Rodwell (Uncle Jim)

JIM

JULY 8, 1944

Dear Rose,

On July 3, I was promoted to Regimental Commander of the 8th Infantry Regiment and I started immediately. Yesterday, commanding the 8th Regiment, I completed one of the most dangerous missions I have been given. It all happened in the vicinity of St. Germain-Sur Seves, France. The area contained a line of marshes that had been flooded by the Germans. Made worse by the rainy weather, the entire area had become a sea of mud. The Germans had also destroyed all the bridges in order to impede our advance and the few roads in the area were muddy or sunken, unable to hold the weight of armored divisions. On top of all this, the area was heavily defended.

Hindered by the swampy area and restricted to a small space, it was decided that the approach could only be pursued by small combat teams. So, at 0345, I was ordered to lead my regimental team through the almost impassable area, slowly and methodically. We struggled to reach a small island in the middle of the swampy, muddy area (an area that was wide open, affording the enemy excellent fields of fire). Yet, in the darkness of morning, and with a careful, steady approach, we advanced to the target.

We attacked enemy units and were under fire the entire time. For many hours, the Germans continued to deliver direct, hostile attack, holding their position on the small island. I went to the 1st Battalion's command post, through enemy fire, so that I could get a clear picture of the attack. I didn't care about what happened to me, I just wanted to help our men succeed. Once I was able to grasp the enemy's hold on the area, I moved from this post to relay the information to my other two Battalion Commanders. This helped us push forward, attacking more units.

Just before dawn, I did the same, this time moving to the 2nd Battalion forward command post to observe the enemy's position and activities. I could make out the artillery, the automatic and small arms fire, even as I was under fire. I felt no fear. I needed to have this information to aid in the success of our assignment, so I just kept moving. There is something within me that is excited when facing danger, rushing into enemy fire, and coming out victorious, leaving enemy targets crumbled and dead in my wake. I don't know why, but I don't feel fear when I am in the midst of battle. I am possessed with a sense of calm; I am unhurried and precise in my decisions. I have difficulty explaining the feelings that seem to wash over me when I am under great pressure.

I then moved among the troops, encouraging them, pushing them forward, helping them to remain calm and brave and focused. We were in this together, Americans fighting the sonsabitches who started this fight. All the while, I was somehow impervious to enemy attack, not hit by a single bullet, not even shrapnel. It was all around me, firing down in all directions, but I was untouched.

At 0730, we had accomplished what we had set out to do, and the enemy units were caught off balance and crushed. We killed just under 500 Germans and captured about 50 prisoners, only suffering four of our own casualties! I think the Germans are starting to realize they are not going to win. They are staying in this fight, but only by sheer guts.

Steadfast and Loyal,
Uncle Jim

~~CONFIDENTIAL~~

```
                                    *Classification cancelled*
                                    *per par 15, AR380-5,     *
                                    *15 March/1944.           *
           HEADQUARTERS             *        WJB              *
        4TH INFANTRY DIVISION       *        AAG              *
           APO 4, US ARMY
```

AG 201-Rodwell, James S. (O)

Subject: Unexpurgated Citation to Award of the Silver Star.

To: Colonel James S. Rodwell, 09663, Cavalry, 8th Infantry.

Citation:

"JAMES S. RODWELL, 09663, Colonel, Cavalry, 8th Infantry, for gallantry in action in the vicinity of St Germain-Sur Seves, France, from 0345 to 0730 on 7 July 1944. The 8th Infantry attacked strong well-emplaced enemy units on an island surrounded by dangerous, almost impassable, swamps which afforded the enemy excellent fields of fire. Displaying extraordinary courage, gallantry, devotion to duty and utter disregard for his own life, Colonel RODWELL, Regimental Commander, 8th Infantry, went to the 1st Battalion forward observation post, and exposing himself to heavy, direct hostile fires, observed the attack and assisted the Battalion Commander in its vigorous prosecution. Later, moving among the troops, Colonel RODWELL'S presence, gallantry and great courage inspired the attacking units to greater effort, coordination and achievement. Shortly after dawn, Colonel RODWELL went to the 2d Battalion forward observation post, and remaining under heavy, direct, observed enemy artillery, automatic, and small arms fires, observed the enemy's position and activities. Colonel RODWELL'S extraordinary courage, gallantry, devotion to duty with utter disregard for his own life and his calm, unhurried leadership, which inspired the troops to greater effort, reflect great credit upon himself and the service."

                                        R. O. BARTON,
                                    Major General, U. S. Army,
                                           Commanding.

Official record for presentation of Silver Star to Uncle Jim, James S. Rodwell, for his leadership on July 7, 1944.

Army released photo of officers and enlisted men receiving Silver Stars (Uncle Jim, first on left)

Uncle Jim giving a speech after receiving Silver Star, Army Signal Corps photo found in Uncle Jim's scrapbook

TEDDY

JULY 9, 1944
JOURNAL — TEDDY ROOSEVELT, JR.

At home in the States, home-front rationing is in effect. Gas, sugar, butter, meat, women's nylons, etc. can only be purchased in small amounts, even if one can afford more. There are different coupons for different types of products. There is uniform rationing which means an equal share of a specific item for all consumers (sugar, for example). There is print rationing to spend on a combination of items (such as cheese or meat). There is differential rationing for products like gasoline. Then, there are items for which an application must be submitted for approval, such as a car or a typewriter, where one must show an absolute need for those items. Car production has been halted for a number of years already so that assembly lines can use steel to focus on building Army vehicles and tanks. Farmers who need to buy tractors are turned down even though they are producing more food than before with fewer workers. It is simply what people are expected to do at home to help the men at war. "Do with less so they'll have more," is the motto.

Rationing for soldiers is a little different though. When we use the word "ration," we mean the types of food we are given to eat.

- "A" ration = fresh food

- "B" ration = packaged food that is not yet prepared, for use in field kitchens
- "C" ration = a meal in a can that is ready to eat, usually meat and beans, meat and hash, or meat and vegetable stew. There is a key on the bottom of the can that you remove and place in the metal opening strip to remove the can's top.
- "D" ration = an emergency bar that has the minimum number of calories needed for one day. These do not taste good, so there is no worry that men will eat them in "non-emergency" situations. In fact, we have nicknamed them, "Hitler's secret weapon," for the effect they often have on our digestive systems.
- "K" ration = survival rations that are complete, packaged meals. There is some sort of canned meat, biscuits, dried fruit bars, and cheese. Also included are: water purification tablets, instant coffee, an orange flavored powdered beverage, caramels or chocolate, toilet paper, chewing gum, and a four-pack of cigarettes for each meal (12 total for the day) with a matchbook. While many of the items are appreciated, we often have to wonder what the processed foods are pretending to be ("Is this supposed to be ham?") and the food is far from tasty. The monotony of K rations can become as grueling as the frontline combat.

When we are able to eat from the field kitchens and have a hot meal prepared by our cooks, there is a noticeable difference. Today the men were issued their first B rations, their first hot meal in over a month (those not directly in the fight, that is). We also enjoyed the orange juice that was sent to us, something we did not drink before the war. I understand that producers in Florida are doing well because of the need to ship citrus fruit for soldiers, in order to prevent scurvy. They are using

German prisoners in POW camps there to help build plants for production. I am sure the prisoners are glad to have something to do and happy to receive the wages required as part of the Geneva Convention guidelines.

After dinner, Roddy and I had a chance to sit and discuss the activities of this war as well as the last, just two war buddies sharing tales of valor, sacrifice, greatness, and sadness. We have very similar thoughts and approaches when it comes to leadership. We both want to be where the action is, with our men, in the line of fire.

I spent several years being criticized for my approach, for leading from the front, for being "too chummy" with my men, but here, under General Barton, it seems to be an accepted leadership style. Since being with the first wave battalions on June 6, I have been more aware of officers doing the same, and it makes me think that it was a minority of superiors who objected to my philosophies. Or perhaps times are changing and attitudes are shifting. Either way, I am encouraged to see more men pushing aside rank in favor of brotherhood on the frontlines.

Roddy, like me, has a complete disregard for his own safety when in battle. We both are at our best under pressure and under fire. Something shifts within and there is an excitement that moves us forward, not even aware of enemy fire raining all around us. Nothing like it. And the first great war was just the beginning. Now, with advances in artillery and military strategy, the adrenaline during battle is even more intense.

I have grown to love Roddy like a brother. We both have lost our own brothers and I think that indistinguishable sadness makes the tie between us stronger, like an unbreakable knot. We understand each other on a different level because we have experienced such tragic loss. Neither can replace the other's sibling, but we come close to filling that void.

Should I lose my life in this conflict while in France, I want to be buried near my brother, Quentin, and I want Roddy to have one of the canes I have used here. In this way, I am with them both, eternally.

JULY 12, 1944
JOURNAL — TEDDY ROOSEVELT, JR.

I am so very tired, but today was a good day. I spent time with the front-line battalions, making the rounds. I like to put chewing gum over the Brigadier General star on my helmet as a symbol of my loyalty to them. In this way, I am not above them in rank, but rather, one of them. I notice it makes them smile when they see it. How foolish it must look, yet how important it is for me to do. I find this provides a sense of calm to the men, showing that I am there with them. I put myself in danger with them, unlike the generals who sit back and watch, giving direction, moving their men like chess pieces from a safe distance. It always fills me with pride to walk among my men, joking with them, and telling them to keep going, telling them, "Don't turn into a target!"

After walking the lines, I had an unexpected visit from my son, Quentin. He told me he had an urge to see me and he traveled a fair distance from his division's area to mine. We met at what I call my "HQ on wheels" so we could spend some time together, alone. My HQ is a German truck captured by one of our units and commandeered to become my private, lovely retreat. My men painted the interior white, and hung an electric light inside to illuminate. There is a bed, a desk, and space for my foot locker. I feel spoiled in the best way.

Quentin and I talked for hours. When we were both in the same division, I suppose I was accustomed to his company. We always knew how to find each other and could visit more often. Now, it is very infrequent. After Quentin landed with the first wave on Omaha beach, while I landed on Utah Beach, it was over a week before I knew he had survived!

Quentin told his own stories of the beach invasion, how he lost all of his equipment in the landing, how he had several hair-raising escapes, and how he learned from that experience and has become more careful since, which made me chuckle. We spoke of home, of our family. He shared his dreams for the future. It was among the best three hours of my entire life, just being together.

I shared with Quentin that I started experiencing some issues with my heart during the invasion on June 6, and how I have become very tired. I'm afraid this cold, damp weather, this constant rain, and the battles of two great wars have put a strain on my old body. Two days ago, the army doctor told me, "Your troubles are primarily from having put an inhuman strain on a machine that is not exactly new." He was trying to be a funny man, but he also states the truth. He gave me something that helps me sleep and that has made a difference the past few nights, yet I am still very tired.

Quentin left shortly before 2200 and it was a pleasing end to a very gratifying day. Now, as I settle in for the night, I can hear the battles raging on in the distance and the firing nearby. The explosions shake the paper on which I write, but the sounds are far enough away to also begin to lull me to sleep. Though I am tired, I am content with the day. I was with the troops I love, a son I love, and now I rest in the truck made for me by the unit I have come to love like family.

Teddy Roosevelt and his son, Quentin

An original copy of a now famous picture of Teddy Roosevelt, found among many of Uncle Jim's mementos. Aunt Polly wrote on the back, "A picture of Gen. Teddy Roosevelt, taken in front of Roddy's command post—the day Gen. Roosevelt died." (This was taken in Meautis, France.)

JIM

JULY 14, 1944

Dear Rose,

Today was the funeral for Ted, just two days after he died, coincidentally on the anniversary of his brother's death in 1918. The ceremony took place at the cemetery at Ste. Mere Eglise and it was a worthy tribute to a great man. I was part of the procession of generals alongside General Patton, General Bradley, General Collins, General Barton, and others. While I would rather my friend was still alive, it was an honor to be included in a way that recognized the kinship between Ted and me.

The band played The Funeral March by Chopin as a division half-track carrying the flag draped casket followed. The men who would carry the casket walked behind. Next came Ted's son, Quentin, and Ted's aides, Stevie and Show. Then followed the procession of Generals and me. Finally, the Honor Company was next, which consisted of one man from each unit in the 4th Infantry Division. Other soldiers from the 4th Infantry Division were present as were many from Ted's beloved 1st Infantry Division, "The Big Red One."

There was a salute from the firing squad for our fallen general and a bugler played Taps. The flag in the cemetery flew at half-mast as the many men who loved Ted stood in respect. We could hear the war carrying on in the distance and this was somehow fitting. Ted would have liked that.

Surrounded by his military family today, just as he was surrounded by us the night he died in his truck, a tribute was paid to a man who was among history's greatest. Had he lived one day longer, he would have come to know of the orders on General Eisenhower's desk that were to give Ted command of a division while recommending a promotion to major general. How bittersweet that the orders could not have been signed just one day sooner so that Ted could die knowing he had risen to that level. He would have been so proud of this accomplishment.

Rose, I have decided to carry the cane Ted gave me throughout the rest of the war. I want to honor him and our friendship in this way. By taking his cane from battle to battle, he is still somehow present. His spirit lives on. It comforts me to feel he is still with me.

My heart is heavy today. My friend is gone, as so many I have loved have gone before.

Steadfast and Loyal,
Uncle Jim

A picture of the funeral procession for Teddy Roosevelt, Jr. on July 14, 1944, Bastille Day. Here, the generals are marching, including General Patton, General Bradley, General Collins, General Barton, and others. Uncle Jim is seen on the right, the second to last in order. He was a colonel when this picture was taken. (Center for Military History)

Beth Rieman is in Delaware, Ohio
August 12, 2018 at 12:00 pm • Delaware, OH

I told you all I had something to share, something I had to figure out HOW to share on here, so here goes...This is a long post, but I don't know how to share our discovery without also giving you some "back story." Feel free to scroll on by if you are not interested, but if you are wanting to hear about the item we found, I think it is important to understand the significance as well as the journey towards discovery...

One person we knew in my grandmother's family was her uncle, James S. Rodwell. Uncle Jim was a decorated war veteran, having fought in both world wars, the second world war with the 4th Infantry Division. This division was the first to arrive on Utah Beach on D-Day and was in the war 199 days straight without rest. This infantry division fought in all the major battles of the European campaign, including the Hürtgen Forest and the Battle of the Bulge.

We knew that Uncle Jim was close friends with Teddy Roosevelt, Jr., the President's son. Teddy was famous in his own right, having posthumously received the Medal of Honor for his leadership on D-Day, as well as four Silver Stars and every other medal that can be awarded. He was the oldest man on D-Day, walking with a cane, swinging it in the air to give directions. There are so many interesting stories about his courage and he sounds like an amazing person.

We knew that Uncle Jim had also received numerous medals for his bravery and my mom had memories of him as a child, but that is all we really knew...until this week when we spent each day researching, going through boxes of family mementos, etc.

My mom had a box with Uncle Jim's most important medals so we started there. We figured out what each was and started to research in order to understand WHY he received these honors. All we could find on the internet was a citation for his Distinguished Service Cross (the second highest honor, second only to the Medal of Honor). Reading about this made Uncle Jim start to come to life for me, but as I searched and searched, I could not find citations for his other medals.

Then we found a scrapbook with the 4th Infantry Division's insignia on it. It was full of newspaper articles and pictures. Every battle he had fought in was documented. If his hometown newspaper wrote an article about an honor he received, it was there! It was a gold mine to me. We learned which battles he earned his medals for and we could follow his path as he moved up through the ranks to Brigadier General. We still couldn't find citations for his medals, though, and I wanted to know WHAT he did to be awarded each medal.

My mom kept saying that she remembered looking through a binder that Uncle Jim put together with papers from his service. She knew that he had the citations in there, but could not remember where she had put it. My dad and I searched the house: bookshelves, closets, storage, even the safe. Nothing.

The next day, I was going through some drawers and stumbled across an old box. When I opened it, it was full of old pictures of my great grandfather (Uncle Jim's brother). We only have one picture of my great-grandfather and thought there were no more in existence because he died very young. My mom asked me to get a chair from the other room so she could sit and go through the box with me. As I got the chair, I looked up and noticed something that seemed "old" on a shelf. I pulled it out...and it was THE BINDER which was full of the Army papers that my uncle had so carefully kept over the years! It was as if the brothers were willing us to find things and working together to help us get to the next step!

When we opened the binder and started going through it, everything fell into place. We found official citations for every medal, each account bringing more tears as we learned about how truly valiant and brave Uncle Jim was. We came across many treasures. One of my favorite pages housed THE actual papers that would have been read as soldiers departed for D Day: Eisenhower's famous address and another announcement from Omar Bradley. I was holding those papers in my hands, the same papers read to Uncle Jim and the other men as they embarked on what must have been a terrifying journey. That left me shaking.

As we kept going through the binder, I found article after article praising Uncle Jim. I felt like I knew him now, like I could tell anyone about him, like I could tell you all his life story. It was incredible. He has left a lasting legacy. That makes my heart so full.

As I was reading the articles, I came across an article about Uncle Jim, written by Ernie Pyle. Ernie Pyle was a famous war correspondent. He embedded himself with various regiments and wrote from the front lines. He won a Pulitzer in 1944 for his work. His columns make you understand truths about war and bring to life the soldiers involved. So, here I am reading a column ABOUT UNCLE JIM that Ernie Pyle wrote! I started crying because it described the way he looked so well. It also included a single sentence that caught my attention: *"He wears a new-type field jacket that fits him like a sack, and he carries a long stick that Teddy Roosevelt gave him."*

Next to this article was placed a famous picture of Teddy Roosevelt, Jr. standing with his cane. On the back of the photo was written, *"A picture of Gen. Teddy Roosevelt, taken in front of Roddy's command post — the day Gen. Roosevelt died."* (My uncle was nicknamed "Roddy" for his last name, Rodwell). I researched to find that this day was July 12, 1944, a little over a month after the D-Day invasion. Brigadier General Teddy Roosevelt, Jr. had been reunited with his son that day and had a heart attack a few hours later. So, this is the last photograph of him alive.

We found a copy of the handwritten letter that Teddy Roosevelt, Jr. wrote, outlining why he should be allowed to go to battle with the first wave on D-Day, after his verbal requests were denied two times. The letter is in HIS HANDWRITING! This was so cool to me and I imagine that Uncle Jim knew it was significant at the time as well, for he took a picture of it and printed it on photo paper.

After that, I found a photograph that must have been taken by Ernie Pyle or his related press. It was of Uncle Jim, seated with some soldiers, going over a map or some plans, perhaps discussing war strategy. He has a cane leaning against the inside of his right thigh. On the back, Uncle Jim's wife had written, *"Note the cane that Teddy Roosevelt gave him."* That detail really touched me. It showed me how close Uncle Jim and Teddy were, how strong their friendship. The cane in the picture was the cane that Ernie Pyle mentioned in his article about Uncle Jim. I read this quote from Ernie Pyle, "The ties that grow between men who live savagely together, relentlessly communing with Death, are ties of great strength. There is a sense of fidelity to each other in a little corps of men who have endured so long, and whose hope in the end can be so small." I think that says it all. It made me cry (once again) to think about how Uncle Jim found a way for his dear friend to be in the war even after his death; he carried that cane with him for the rest of the battles and, in that way, Teddy was still with him.

All of this was enough to leave me in awe. But there was more…

Then, my mom said, "You guys…I think we have that cane!"

Silence.

Astonishment.

A little doubt.

"Grandma moved a cane with her and I thought it was odd because it is something that looks like she should have thrown it out with some of the other belongings that didn't make the move. She said it belonged to her Uncle Jim and that it was very special to her. Uncle Jim never walked with a cane, so I thought this was odd. Grandma was given the cane with his medals, the scrapbook, and the binder, all together after Uncle Jim died."

My dad sprung up and knew where to look. He had almost used the cane as firewood because he thought nothing of its significance. He brought the cane into the room and we examined it. We compared it to pictures and figuratively checked all the boxes to determine provenance. And then we realized it…we had THE cane! THE CANE that belonged to Teddy Roosevelt, Jr.! THE CANE that was with him in Normandy and was given to Uncle Jim while he was there! THE CANE that my uncle continued to carry throughout all the major battles in WWII. YOU GUYS, WE HAD TEDDY ROOSEVELT, JR's CANE!!!! This was as much a part of his "being" as the stove-pipe hat was Lincoln's. AND WE HAD IT IN OUR POSSESSION!!!! He is known for storming Utah Beach on D-Day with a cane in his hand, and this was one of his canes, perhaps even the same cane!

It was awesome in the true sense of the word to grip the handle and know that Teddy Roosevelt, Jr. and Uncle Jim had done the same. To walk carefully with it and imagine all the places it had been. To touch the bottom and wonder if it had touched the sand on Utah Beach. To walk with it and know that it was in France, at the liberation of Paris, in the bloody Hürtgen Forest, at the Battle of the Bulge, and brought back to the United States as a personal reminder of the war, of its owner, and of a great friendship. Just absolutely incredible. I cry typing this. The emotions of that week spent learning about Uncle Jim and his division had come full circle and I was holding a piece of history.

134 | ELIZABETH RIEMAN

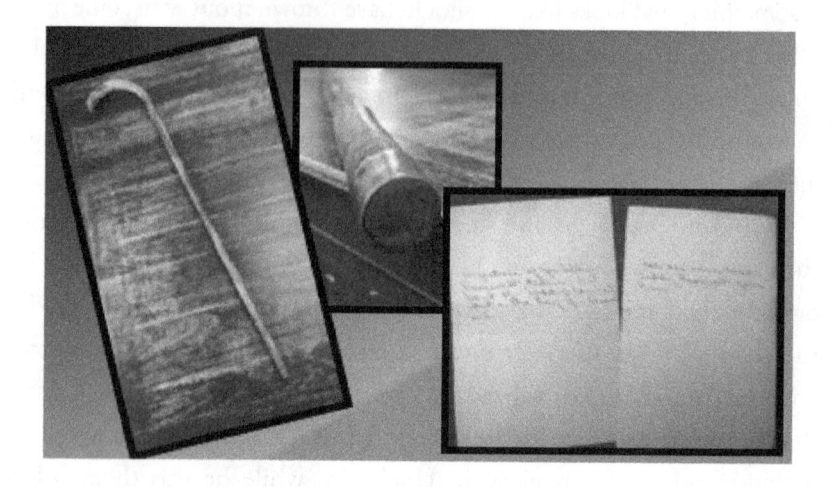

The cane. There is a concave mark on the base where a spiked appendage has worn off.

Picture of Uncle Jim (far right, hand on chin) with the cane resting on his right leg. On the back, Aunt Polly wrote, "Notice the cane that Teddy Roosevelt gave him."

FAME: One of the newest and most popular books to come direct from the fighting fronts practically tells the day-by-day "work" of a Valley service man over a period of some weeks last summer. It is Ernie Pyle's "Brave Men" and one section of it deals in detail of the activities of a unit commanded by Gen. R. S. Rodwell, who was a colonel at the time the articles were written. Mrs. Rodwell is a Mission girl, the former Miss Pauline Drummond, who is now spending the duration in Rio Grande (which they consider their home), every word Pyle has written about "Roddy" is packed with interest for their Valley friends and relatives.

Newspaper clipping found with Ernie Pyle's article about Uncle Jim in his scrapbook

JIM

JULY 20, 1944

Dear Rose,

The famous Ernie Pyle is with us as part of his rotation as a war correspondent. I am sure you have seen some of his columns in the papers back home. His stories actually moved Congress to pass a bill last May that gave combat soldiers more pay -the influence of his stories is truly that significant. He writes stories that give the people back home a glimpse of our experiences as soldiers and his honesty affects change in policy. How many writers can say that, I wonder?

Ernie has been given complete freedom to do what he needs to do and to interview whomever he wishes. Additionally, as a correspondent, he can also leave the front whenever he wants, unlike an enlisted man (though, truly, he does put himself at risk to write his stories). That is why I have nicknamed him "The General," and the name makes him smile. He wrote a column about me, but it will not use my name due to security blackouts. Look for a column about an Army colonel who has "Mongolian face." You will have to share your opinion with me once you have read it. He sure did capture my appearance in a way I had not thought of myself, but I'm afraid the story makes me come across a little more boorish than I really am. The personality he portrays is accurate for when I am briefing men and leading them into the front, though. One cannot be too soft in those moments, and I am not one for eloquent speeches. The men here are good-naturedly teasing me about "The General's" characterization of my crusty personality, but I am very honored to have been the subject of one of his columns.

Ernie gets in with the men on the front lines. He eats the same rations they eat, sleeps in the same uncomfortable environments, and takes meaning and understanding away from the interactions he has with them. In this way, he gains a familiarity, an empathy, for the life of a soldier. Unarmed, he goes into battle with us and risks his life to be able to report about the war with complete accuracy.

Then, when he is ready to write, you will find him somewhere by himself, away from the tents, slightly removed but still in our vicinity. He assembles a military folding table and creates an "office space" on which to write. Coffee in one corner, notes in the other, a cigarette dangling from his lips, he removes his typewriter from its case and begins to write. In soldiers' garb, with his goggles pushed above the rim of his woolen cap, it is like he is mining for the perfect words, on a mission to help his readers feel closer to the men they are missing, the men who are sacrificing for others' freedom. I have a lot of respect for Ernie Pyle.

"The General" writes about the common man in this war, raw and candid. He is not like other correspondents who write broadly about the war, who describe the battles using a wide lens. He narrows his focus and sends home stories about the human parts that are the foundation of war. While others write about tanks moving over difficult terrain and the battles they witness, he writes about the bloody helmet lying in the middle of the field. His stories truly capture the essence of this war and the men who are fighting in it. If you have not read any of his columns, please make sure you do. And look for the story about the Colonel with the Mongolian eyes!

Steadfast and Loyal,
Uncle Jim

This Commander Realizes the Main Business in War Is to Kill the Enemy

By ERNIE PYLE

ON THE WESTERN FRONT (by wireless)— The commander of the particular regiment of the Fourth Infantry Division that we have been with is one of my favorites.

That's partly because he flatters me by calling me "General," partly because just looking at him makes me chuckle to myself, and partly because I think he's a very fine soldier.

Security forbids my giving his name. He is a Regular Army colonel and he was overseas in the last war. His division commander says the only trouble with him is that he's too bold, and if he isn't careful he's liable to get clipped one of these days.

He is rather unusual looking. There is something almost Mongolian about his face. When cleaned up he could be a Cossack. When tired and dirty he could be a movie gangster. But either way, his eyes always twinkle.

He has a facility for direct thought that is unusual. He is impatient of thinking that gets off onto by-ways.

He has a little habit of good-naturedly reprimanding people by cocking his head over to one side, getting his face below yours and saying something sharp, and then looking up at you with a quizzical smirk like a laughing cat.

* * *

ONE day I heard him ask a battalion commander what his position was. The battalion commander started going into details of why his troops hadn't got as far as he had hoped. The colonel cocked his head over, squinted up at the battalion commander, and said:

"I didn't ask you that. I asked you where you were."

(Continued on Page 22)

Battle Commander

By Ernie Pyle

(Continued from Page 2)

The colonel goes constantly from one battalion to another during battle, from early light till darkness. He wears a new-type field jacket that fits him like a sack, and he carries a long stick that Teddy Roosevelt gave him. He keeps constantly prodding his commanders to push hard, not to let up, to keep driving and driving.

He is impatient with commanders who lose the main point of the war by getting involved in details—the main point, of course, being to kill Germans. His philosophy of war is expressed in the simple formula of "shoot the sonsabitches."

Once I was at a battalion command post when we got word that 60 Germans were coming down the road in a counterattack. Everybody got excited. They called the colonel on a field phone, gave him the details and asked him what to do. He had the solution in a nutshell.

He just said, "Shoot the sonsabitches," and hung up.

* * *

ANOTHER of my favorites is a sergeant who runs the colonel's regimental mess. He cooks some himself, but mostly he bosses the cooking.

His name is Charles J. Murphy, and his home is at Trenton, N. J. Murphy is red-headed, but has his head nearly shaved like practically all the Western Front soldiers—officers as well as men. Murph is funny, but he seldom smiles.

When I asked him what he did in civilian life, he thought a moment and then said: "Well, I was a shyster. Guess you'd call me a kind of promoter. I always had the kind of job where you made $50 a week salary and $1500 on the side."

"How's that for an honest man?"

Murph and I got to talking about newspapermen one day. Murph said his grandfather was a newspaperman. He retired in old age and lived in Murph's house.

"My grandfather went nuts reading newspapers," Murph said. "It was a phobia with him. Every day he'd buy $1.50 worth of 2-cent newspapers and then read them all night.

"He wouldn't read the ads. He would just read the stories, looking for something to criticize. He'd get fuming mad.

"Lots of times when I was a kid he'd get me out of bed at 2 or 3 in the morning and point to some story in the paper and rave about reporters who didn't have sense enough to put a period at the end of a sentence."

Murph and I agreed that it was fortunate his grandfather passed on before he got to reading my stuff, or he would doubtless have run amuck.

Murph never smoked cigarets until he landed in France on D-Day, but now he smokes one after another. He is about the tenth soldier who has told me that same thing. A guy in war has to have some outlet for his nerves, and I guess smoking is as good as anything.

* * *

ALL kinds of incongruous things happen during a battle. For instance, during one lull I got my portrait painted in water color. The artist sat cross-legged on the grass and it took about an hour.

The painter was Pfc. Leon Wall, from Wyoming, Pa. He went to the National Academy of Design in New York for six years, did research for the Metropolitan Museum and lectured on art at the New York World's Fair.

Artist Wall is now, of all things, a cook and KP in an infantry regiment mess. He hasn't done any war paintings at all since the invasion. I asked him why not. He said: "Well, at first I was too scared, and since then I've been too busy."

Ernie Pyle article, published in newspapers throughout the U.S., August 1944, copy found among Uncle Jim's mementos

JULY 26, 1944

Dear Rose,

Yesterday was another day spent in France that I will never forget! It was a day that could have ended much differently, with a lot more casualties, but that was not the case! Thank God we were able to take a situation that was out of our control, react quickly, and regroup so that our mission could go off as planned.

I was in command of the 8th Infantry Regiment of our 4th Infantry Division and we were charged to spearhead a breakthrough in a vital sector near St. Lo, creating a protected corridor through which additional forces would advance. We were to begin our attack at 1100 hours, following an hour and a quarter of Allied bombing that had started at 0900 hours in preparation for our advance. Plans were in place for bombs to be dropped on the enemy where they were entrenched east of the Perrieres Highway, an area that needed to be cleared of the Germans.

This is something new the Army is trying: the use of heavy bombers in advance of ground combat troops. The bombings are designed to disorganize the enemy. They halt counterattacks while also removing artillery or reserve support from various areas on their front line. Disorganizing the Germans leaves only small pockets of effective resistance for our men to fight.

Unfortunately, we didn't anticipate some of the possible pitfalls. The Perrieres Highway was set as a marker for the Allied plane bombings, but the clouds of dust kicked up from the bombs made the line invisible to pilots. As our regiment approached our mark, pilots couldn't see their highway mark through the dust and they were dropping bombs mostly blindly. Many bombs were falling short of the release line, therefore, falling on friendly troops. That's right, Allied planes were dropping bombs on us, mistakenly! An entire battalion of another division was wiped out, all men except the commander killed. A Lieutenant General, who was only observing the battle, was blown into the air and his flesh was strewn in the field; his death was only confirmed when a scrap of his uniform was found and the stars on the shoulder could serve as identification.

All four of our regiment's assault companies were bombed! In one company, when the bombs dropped, several men were literally buried alive, so deep they had to be dug out. All around, men were visibly shaken, some near hysteria. This was mass chaos and I could see the dire consequences of what was happening.

We set off orange smoke to alert air support of our location, but it was not seen and the bombing continued. Some of these bombs fell into our lines, killing some of the men and scattering the others. Several of the men lost contact with their organizations, several were disoriented, most were losing confidence. My unit was wavering and my men were not safe. The ground shook as bombs were exploding all around our command post and men were panicking. I encountered men who were in complete shock, in a daze, staring blankly; they were completely unable to understand anything I said to them. Our telephone lines went out and I could not communicate with other positions.

All I could think of was my men's safety. Without considering the danger, I left my command post and made my way along the open road while others were forced to take cover, friendly bombs dropping on either side of me and heavy enemy fire coming at me. I found some men running to the wrong areas, some men wounded and lost, and others confused and rattled. I moved among them to direct those who were still able to fight back to their companies while telling the others to remain under cover. I ordered the wounded to medical stations.

Meanwhile, the officers I had left back at the command post started to organize and form a new plan, sure there was no way we could perform our original mission. They assumed I would not make it back alive, and had stepped into leadership roles. Surprised to see me upon my return, they cautioned against moving ahead with the original mission. I was not of the same opinion and believed that a delayed attack on our end would negatively affect all future offensive plans. We had to adjust the original plan, but the mission needed to continue on time.

I repositioned attack units, moved one company to set up anti-tank positions, moved another to be immediately ready for defensive fire, and moved my command post to a forward position. Suggestions were made to move reserves to the front, but there was no time for that. We organized the existing troops to be quickly battle ready. Once everyone was assembled, I knew I had to restore courage and confidence. My adrenaline rushing, I gave the men a short pep talk, looked at my watch (1057), and told them to kill the sonsabitches! I rushed to the troops on the frontline to rally the men for the attack. Miraculously, we attacked at 1100 hours, as scheduled!

Taking advantage of the bombings, we moved so quickly that we stunned the already confused Germans right out of their foxholes and the battle raged on. I left my position and began to move to 2nd Battalion's Command Post. I was about to cross a hedgerow, when suddenly I saw a group of about a dozen or so Germans who were moving into abandoned foxholes with their weapons. I had to think quickly as I had no backup and was outnumbered. I leaped over the hedgerow and yelled, "Halt!" The Germans, seeing an older officer instead of a young soldier, assumed they were surrounded and that I was simply the person in charge of their capture. They immediately dropped their weapons accordingly, so I gathered the weapons, rounded up the men, and took them with me to the command post. They were surprised to discover that I was alone, and that they were not actually surrounded. I was surprised that I made it out alive.

We carried on the fight and gained high ground just before dark when we were ordered to dig in for the night. General Barton did not want us to risk advancing through a town at night where Germans could hide in buildings and behind obstacles, where the roads are narrow for moving tanks and other vehicles, and wherein doing so meant losing our advantage with the high ground we had gained. He also knew that the troops had been fighting non-stop and were exhausted, hungry, and mentally drained from the chaos of the day. So, we settled in for the night, knowing that, in spite of the disruption in our original plan, we were successful in breaking through the main line of resistance, on time, leaving it open for the next penetration.

I am proud of my men. They were shaken by friendly fire and were operating understrength when attacking, but they were determined and aggressive. A lesser regiment would have advanced behind schedule and with less success. We have certainly been learning, since day one of this invasion, that plans can look good on paper in a manual, but almost every time, we have to be ready for the unexpected, ready to adjust and reorganize in order to accomplish our objectives. Ernie Pyle was with us, in the danger of it all, and he wrote about it: "The great Allied breakthrough on July 25, spearheaded by three infantry divisions with the 4th Infantry Division in the center of the thrust, would go down as one of the greatest historical dates of WWII." I wish Ted had been there to see it. I wish Ted had been there to see it. (though his cane was there with me, so, in a way, he was.)

Steadfast and Loyal,
Uncle Jim

Official record for presentation of Oak-Leaf Cluster to Silver Star to James S. Rodwell for his leadership on July 25, 1944.

Armed with only a leather-handled cane, a regimental commander captured 12 German prisoners near Notre Dame ée Couilly.

Accompanied by his jeep driver, Sgt. Ransyom Clark, of Charleston, S C., and Sgt. Ralph S. Maretto, of Garfield, N J. the colonel sighted the Nazi soldiers while trying to locate a forward OP near the front.

The colonel and the two enlisted men jumped a hedgerow and ordered the Nazis to surrender and they then marched the prisoners back to a command post.

Article about St. Lo, found in Uncle Jim's scrapbook. I love knowing that he had the cane with him in battle. He originally wrapped the cane handle in leather so that he would have a loop to hang on his wrist in order to keep his hands free.

Beth Rieman is in Delaware, Ohio

August 13, 2018 at 12:00 pm • Delaware, OH

A few days ago, I received an email from the museum at Utah Beach in France. The ball is rolling!

> Dear Madam,
>
> I would like to thank you about your wish to donate to our Utah Beach Landing Museum the Cane brought by Brigadier General Theodore Roosevelt during WWII, and especially on D Day until the day he gave it to your uncle on 12th July 1944. It is very emotional that General Roosevelt gave it to your uncle the day he died from heart brake attack.
>
> You can be certain that the cane – that is historically an important artifact for us – would be in very good place, in the showcases dedicated to the 4th Infantry Division.
>
> We are proud to accept to receive it, and also the newspaper article written by Ernie Pyle and photographies about the 4th Infantry Division. Also, do you want to tell the war story of your uncle during WWII, and especially since the D Day landing at Utah Beach ?
>
> Waiting to read you again,
>
> With my Kindest Regards,
>
> Benoît
>
> Responsable des Recherches Historiques et des Collections

JIM

AUGUST 16, 1944

Dear Rose,

Today, after General Barton was awarded both the Distinguished Service Cross and a Silver Star, after the Distinguished Service Cross was awarded to Arthur Teague, John Welborn, and George Mabry as well, 45 were awarded the Silver Star, and Combat Infantryman Badges were also awarded. I was one of the many who were awarded the Combat Infantryman's Badge (CIB). This is a new award, not bestowed upon soldiers in the last war. It was created just a year ago, as a way to honor the infantry soldier who fights a ground fight, close to the enemy, and whose branch, therefore, suffers the most casualties.

Ernie Pyle wrote, "I love the infantry because they are the underdogs. They are the mud-rain-frost-and-wind boys. They have no comforts, and they even learn to live without necessities. And in the end, they are the guys the wars can't be won without." He is exactly right on every level. We like to say that, for every one infantry soldier, there is the backing of ten other soldiers, from other branches, in rear support. The CIB recognizes this.

Because of the dangers faced by an infantry soldier who engages on foot, knowing the likelihood of death when fighting the enemy head on, many times attracting fire just to make room for other soldiers to advance, ours is the only branch of the military that has been granted an award like this (though I wager the other branches will push to have their own in the future). In order to receive a CIB, a soldier must participate in active, ground combat with direct fires. One must fight directly, in harm's way; he cannot simply be part of a unit that was engaged in combat, he has to be involved in the combat.

This badge carries a lot of prestige for myself and the many men who were awarded the CIB today. The musket mounted on a blue rectangular field then resting on a laurel wreath is a symbol to ourselves and others that we are the men to whom Ernie is referring, the men on whose backs the war is won. The CIB will be pinned on uniforms, above all others, to show how we are willing to die so that others may live. I feel honored to have received it today, along with other soldiers and only two other officers: Colonel Charles T. Lanham and Colonel James S. Luckett, the other two Regimental commanders. Other officers and men were awarded the CIB in battalion and company formations.

Steadfast and Loyal,
Uncle Jim

UNPACKING YESTERDAY | 151

Picture of Uncle Jim receiving Combat Infantryman's Badge, General Barton, pinning it on. Photo found in Uncle Jim's scrapbook

AUGUST 30, 1944

Dear Rose,

Paris is liberated! Just days before the liberation, through driving rain, the capitol was still surrounded. Therefore, as a division, our regiments moved in different directions :the 12th Infantry Regiment pushed into Paris, the 22nd Infantry Regiment followed, and my 8th Infantry Regiment went around the center of the city, through the suburbs. In this way, the combined regiments of the 4th Infantry Division led the fight to victory, our division the first Allied force into the city! (We were the first on the beach on D-Day and now first into Paris!)

Once it was clear that Paris was no longer in the hands of the enemy, the German general would not surrender without a show of arms. So he was allowed to go back into position while the French 2nd Armored Division pointed their weapons in his direction and aimed to miss. It seemed like a ridiculous spectacle, but as long as he surrendered, I suppose it didn't hurt to allow him to do so with a staged sense of pride.

Following the surrender, under the Arch de Triomph, a wreath was laid on the Tomb of the Unknown Soldier, buried after the last great war. It was a quiet moment: no speeches, just silent respect. I think all involved were filled with thoughts of how much we had seen in just over two months, since our landing on Utah Beach: brutal fighting, German surrenders, and so many men lost. When coupled with the disheartening realization that our countries had now fought on this soil twice in the same lifetime, the moment became a bit somber.

We did not get to stay long and we did not get to see the grand celebration that followed this somber moment. We were tasked to move through Paris in pursuit of the Germans through France, pushing towards Belgium. What it must have been like to be in Paris following her liberation, though! The stories I have heard since are nothing short of extraordinary!

When we were heading out of Paris, other divisions started to move through the city. Thousands of citizens lined the avenue of the Champs d'Elysee and cheered as General Charles de Gaulle and the American 30th Infantry Division marched in triumph. Thousands of American doughboys passed by a flag draped stand that held high ranking American and French officers. The band played marches for both countries while planes slowly circled overhead.

I hear it took hours for soldiers to move through the streets! The people of France laid flowers on their tanks, jeeps, and half-tracks. Everywhere they heard cries of, "Merci! Viva la Ameriques!" Old men saluted. Young men vigorously shook soldiers' hands and patted their backs. Girls gave hugs and covered GIs in kisses. Mothers handed their babies to GIs to kiss and encouraged their daughters to find romantic connections. Many young girls were seen crawling into tank hatches by day and sneaking out of soldiers' pup tents in the morning (I wonder if the hospitals of Paris will see a surge in births next spring!)

Soldiers were given wine, freshly baked bread, even fresh vegetables! It has been a long time since any of us have eaten vegetables! Vegetables from gardens! Fresh, ripe vegetables! I can almost taste them myself, hearing the stories. Soldiers made salads in their helmets, like giant mixing bowls, and ate right out of them while they marched down the streets. It sounds like the whole day was one big party and that everyone was so happy. It makes me happy to know that there were so many smiles on the faces of men who had faced unimaginable horrors leading up to that day.

It would have been nice to celebrate along with the other soldiers, to rejoice in the victory, but the war is not over and we had to continue our fight against the enemy. Even without partaking in the celebration, that day of liberation gave us a huge boost in morale. Hearing the news of the celebration and seeing the French flag flying in Paris for the first time in a very long time was all the reward we needed. This is exactly why we are here and we know we are accomplishing the job we came here to do.

Steadfast and Loyal,
Uncle Jim

154 | ELIZABETH RIEMAN

Newspaper clippings found in Uncle Jim's scrapbook

SEPTEMBER 1, 1944

Dear Rose,

I have to write to you about Ernest Hemingway. He came to Europe as a war correspondent and has recently attached himself to the 4th Infantry Division, following us as we fight the enemy. He is a welcome addition, bringing with him a mystique that comes from his prestige as a famous author as well as his bigger- than-life personality. He is magnetic and everyone enjoys his presence. He makes us all laugh and tells stories that are as grand as you would expect them to be, just like the stories he writes.

General Barton gave Hemingway a driver, "Red" Pelkey, who is nicknamed for—you guessed it—his red hair. Red drives Hemingway anywhere he wants to go, at any time. The two are very free-spirited and enjoy traveling through France on the roads for which Hemingway developed a familiarity when he was here during the last war. We smile when we see them zipping along together.

I think Hemingway would rather be a general than a war correspondent. There are laws governing correspondents, and one of the rules is that they are not to engage in any combat or carry/use any weapons. This does not matter to Hemingway. He does not want to sit back and watch the war; he wants to take part in it. When accused by others of breaking this rule, even when reprimanded by generals, Hemingway just denies having done so. And that is that. No more questions asked. It makes us all laugh—that confident, "stick-it-to-em" nature that epitomizes Hemingway.

Recently, Hemingway decided that he would form his own little regiment of rag-tag followers which he calls his "Band of Irregulars." The regiment consists of a cook, a camp photographer, an army historian—you get the idea. They go around each night harassing any small groups of defeated Germans they can find, Hemingway and Red zipping around on an abandoned German motorcycle and side-car they commandeered. One evening, Hemingway and Red filled the sidecar with grenades and moved through a village looking for Germans. They were told there might be some Germans in the cellar of a nearby house, so they took the pins from three grenades, shouted a warning, and threw the grenades down the cellar stairs. No one knows if there really were any men in that cellar, but the story is that Hemingway mopped up a whole group of Nazis and was a hero to the villagers!

I think Hemingway thinks of war as a great sport, like hunting deer. One day, while on the hunt, his motorcycle sidecar full of champagne and machine guns, Hemingway was thrown off the motorcycle when a shell exploded ten yards away. He ended up in a muddy ditch, face down for several hours, listening for the danger to pass. As soon it had, Hemingway sat up, and yelled at the photographer who was with him, sure he had been standing by to be the first to take a picture of Hemingway's dead body. There are many stories like this, where Hemingway escapes death and either loses his temper and directs anger at one of the people around him, or calmly swigs booze from his canteen, as if he had not just watched his life pass before his eyes. I just laugh to myself over the images I have in my mind of this story, and so many others belonging to him. I think we all wish we had a little of his personality within us: that assured, unaffected attitude that embodies Hemingway.

When we were moving into Paris, Hemingway and Red broke off from our division and took an alternate route in a race to liberate the city. They traveled on hidden roads while swigging booze, enjoying the ride. I think the enjoyment delayed them a little because they did not make it to Paris in time to receive the honor of liberating the city, but Hemingway and his friends did liberate the wine cellar of the Ritz hotel. They celebrated for days on end, gorging themselves on Parisian food and liquor. This caused an international incident, but we have sort of come to expect there to be a big story whenever Hemingway is involved. Hemingway, the armed correspondent, is fighting his own war right now and enjoying every minute. I have to tell you, we of the 4th Infantry Division are thoroughly enjoying it as well!

Steadfast and Loyal,
Uncle Jim

Ernest Hemingway (JFK Presidential Library and Museum, Boston)

SEPTEMBER 14, 1944

Dear Rose,

We continue to make more progress as we advance across Europe. On September 11, our division was the first to drive a wedge through the Siegfried Line and were the first into Germany! First on the beach, first into Paris, and now first into Germany! And, to top it off, we are ahead of schedule!

This is particularly rewarding because we were fighting against excellent defenses when we pushed into Germany. Hitler called in all available forces and was certain we would not break through his line. They had been preparing for this for four years, were trained and readied for this, and had even built defenses that should have stopped us.

We encountered heavy resistance at every turn. There were "dragons' teeth" in many areas, which are huge concrete barriers, shaped like triangles. They are dug deep into the ground with just the points sticking out, like teeth. They can stop armored divisions. The Germans also had rows of bunkers that were made with thick concrete walls and steel doors; the bunkers were covered with vegetation as camouflage and had many chambers inside. From these bunkers, the Germans had an advantage because they could fire at us from behind those six-foot thick walls while remaining protected.

When weaker forces could have been annihilated, we were not. All of their preparation, all of their obstacles, and all of their power were no match for us. Now we can push deeper into Germany where the enemy will surely be preparing a major defense of their homeland.

There is an infantry saying, "It is all over but the fighting." It is all over for the enemy.

Steadfast and Loyal,
Uncle Jim

P.S. I have to tell you another recent story about Ernest Hemingway. He was hosting a dinner during which a German shell shook the house and destroyed a wall in the very room where Hemingway and his guests sat. All the guests immediately fell to the floor and took cover. Hemingway, however, was the only person left sitting at the table where he continued to stab at a piece of steak with his fork, as if nothing had just happened. If this doesn't exemplify the Hemmingway I have come to know, I don't know what does!

Gigantic Battle Shapes Up On Siegfried Line

9-7-44

LONDON —(Æ)— The American First and Third armies hammered eastward on two broad fronts toward Germany today, heading for the Siegfried Line where a decisive battle, perhaps the last great battle of the war in Europe, may be fought.

Lt. Gen. George S. Patton's Third Army, moving up to the Moselle river on a front of more than 50 miles from Luxembourg to Nancy, wedged into the outskirts of the fortress city of Metz on the river's east bank. They had won one costly bridgehead across the Moselle.

Attacking both north and south of Metz, the Americans ran into fierce artillery fire as Nazi resistance stiffened under orders to hold out to the last in a desperate time-gaining buffer stand in front of the menaced Siegfried line.

Front line dispatches said there had been no additional crossings on the Moselle since the Americans breached the river in strength yesterday after a week's

Newspaper clipping found in Uncle Jim's scrapbook

Beth Rieman is in Delaware, Ohio
August 29, 2018 at 12:00 pm • Delaware, OH

I don't know who will go (or when), but it is happening! The cane is making its way to France!!!

> **Benoît**
> to me, Séverine
> 2:28 AM View details
>
> Dear Madam,
>
> Yesterday morning, I talked to my director and the mayor about how to do to help you for your travel that you plan for next year, with the idea to donate to the museum the BG Theodore Roosevelt 's canne.
>
> And we have one solution to suggest to you. But I believe that is to my director – Mrs Séverine Letourneur Diaz – to explain to you, that's why I send this email to her also.
>
> I think she will email you during this week.
>
> Waiting to meet you and your family next year, I wish you a nice day !
>
>
> With my Kindest Regards,
>
>
> Benoît

Screenshot of email from Utah Beach Museum

Utah Beach Museum

Séverine [redacted]
to me

Wed, Aug 29, 2018, 10:39 AM

Dear Madam,

First of all I would like to thank you for your interest in the Utah Beach Museum. I followed your conversations with Benoit and I want to tell you how honored we are that you thought of our Museum to donate BG Theodore Roosevelt's cane.
We understand the difficulty and the financial cost of traveling in France, that's why we would be delighted to offer you a ticket from the United States as well as the pick-up from Paris to bring you Normandy.
Do not hesitate to contact me if you have additional questions.
Best regards.

Screenshot of second email from Utah Beach Museum

JIM

SEPTEMBER 17, 1944

Dear Rose,

It won't be much longer now. We are moving so quickly that our supply units can't keep up with us. I even saw a note to cancel the order for winter clothing and boots in order to get other supplies to the troops quickly. We are certain we will be home before Christmas so we won't need winter supplies, and it would be better to get food, ammunition, and gasoline sooner.

Home before Christmas! I have been thinking about what I want to do on my first day at home, when this war is over. I dream about it, actually, when I have time to sleep long enough to dream.

First, I want to take a long, hot shower. Twice. Shave with a thick lather and a sharp blade. Dress in clean cotton pajamas that have been hung on the line to dry. Then I want to read and nap in bed with freshly cleaned sheets, fluffy pillows, and a soft blanket. When I wake, I would like to dress to go to the club for cocktails and dinner with Aunt Polly and our friends. I will order all the favorites from upstate New York: either scalloped oysters or prime rib (maybe both!), salt potatoes, and a double order of fresh vegetables. For dessert: grape pie! After dinner, I want to go on a stroll with Aunt Polly, hold her hand, and talk about anything but the war. Then we can have a nightcap at home before returning to the comfort of that big, luxurious bed where I will sleep until morning without setting an alarm.

It may seem simple, but aside from you and loved ones, these are the things I miss most—the everyday comforts and pleasures of home.

Steadfast and Loyal,
Uncle Jim

OCTOBER 15, 1944

Dear Rose,

I had a very brief transfer to the 9th Infantry Division from late September until October 6. It all happened quickly and I barely had any time to orient myself to the 9th Infantry Division before being reassigned back to the 4th Infantry Division! It all started after I wrote the last letter, on September 17, when General Barton was on his way to visit my 8th Infantry Regiment command post in Rodscheid. While on his way, Barton's jeep came under heavy artillery fire. He had to dismount and take cover until, after a brief lull, he got back in and made a run for it. He was able to reach our post and stayed until morning, but not without his ulcer aggravating him more than usual.

The following evening, Barton received a call from the Corps Commander and was told to report to the 44th Evacuation Hospital and meet with the army surgeon. Barton objected, but he was told that it was not negotiable. When Barton met with the surgeon, he was ordered to take six weeks rest. That truly did not go over well with Barton! He protested profusely, but got nowhere. He was sent to Paris to report to the American Hospital there.

As Barton began treatment, I received word that I was to report to the 9th Infantry Division with a promotion to Assistant Division Commander, Colonel McKee taking over my position as commander of the 8th Infantry Regiment in our 4th Infantry Division. This was a lot for me to take in all at once: losing Barton and losing my place with the 4th Infantry Division. Don't get me wrong, I am proud to receive a promotion, but the change was very sudden and the 4th Infantry Division was hard to leave. This division is my family.

So there we were, Tubby and me, separated from each other and separated from our beloved division. He spent his days in Paris, receiving division reports, mail, and orders, all the while begging to be given a quick release. I spent my time acquainting myself with a new position and a new division. The 9th Infantry Division was in the heat of combat and I jumped into preparation and planning for an attack on Germeter and Vosseneck, part of the Hürtgen Forest. We were to jump off on October 5, but that was postponed for 24 hours and I was called back to the 4th Infantry Division, before I could see the plan of attack under way.

As it turns out, Tubby's six weeks of prescribed rest lasted just over two weeks and he was reassigned on October 4, after begging throughout his hospital stay. When he reported back to the 4th Infantry Division and realized I had been transferred, a new commander of the 8th Infantry Regiment assigned in my absence, he insisted that I return and that I be reassigned as the Assistant Division Commander, now of the 4th Infantry Division (the position once held by Ted). By noon on October 7, I was with the 4th Infantry Division again. I had dinner that evening with Tubby and everything fell back into place. I was glad for the return to our division.

I have learned that the attack on Germeter and Vosseneck, which I was helping to plan, had I stayed with the 9th Infantry Division, was brutal. Fighting in the Hürtgen Forest was like being fed to a meat grinder and the number of casualties incurred (as well as other losses due to trench foot, sickness, injury, and mental issues) were immense. The only winner in that place was the forest as it devoured the men who entered.

Steadfast and Loyal,
Uncle Jim

Uncle Jim with Colonel Richard McKee, upon Uncle Jim's return to the 4th Infantry Division where McKee was now commanding the 8th Infantry Regiment, October 1944 (Uncle Jim is holding the cane) 4th Infantry Division archives

OCTOBER 20, 1944

Dear Rose,

We have many assault weapons at our disposal but we also have another weapon: propaganda. We have airborne units assigned specifically to this task. Leaflets are dropped from open hatches or from "leaflet bombers" which open mid-air to circulate materials. This gets around radio jamming and counteracts the enemy's fabrications as we send messages to civilians. Especially at the start of our engagement, we needed to drop information in areas where civilians were cut off from the world and were only fed German "news." When we drop leaflets with the enemy in mind, though, we are trying to decrease resistance and increase the likelihood of surrenders.

This is not an idea that is only reserved for the Allied Army. The enemy is spending plenty of money and time doing the same on their end, trying to influence the thoughts of our soldiers. Our men have found many of their leaflets, but they are not affected. One of the soldiers in Company G has been collecting German propaganda. His collection has served as a source of entertainment during our periods of boredom. It is interesting to analyze the enemy's approach in comparison to our government's ideas.

The German leaflets play on a soldier's basic worries. "Will your mother be a gold star mother?" accompanies a picture of a woman, sobbing over her son's grave. "Two years is a long time to wait!" runs above a picture of a woman back home in the arms of an older man (who has stereotypically Jewish features, by the way). They even have an entire series called, "The Girl You Left Behind" which has various scenes of wives and girlfriends finding new romantic interests and sending "Dear John letters" overseas to the soldiers who love them. One such scene is a young girl who has taken a job in a store with an older gentleman as her boss; it shows him lifting the hem of her dress to touch her leg and has a message about a wealthy business owner making the moves on a soldier's fiancé. On a less shocking note, there are also leaflets where a soldier is kissing the love of his life and the message is that she is not doing well at home without him, that she is sad because so many are already dead. They even drop notes to tell soldiers that "All German POW camps are run on the Geneva Convention Plan" in hopes that they will surrender.

The Allied airborne leaflets are more about intimidation. We drop surrender leaflets and provide instructions for deserting the German Army. We drop a four-page booklet that is about our plans for complete annihilation of the enemy. One of our leaflets has a picture of an open field that is lined with thousands of German graves. We have even predated documents to look like government classified intel containing Allied "secrets" which, if the enemy soldier believes them, will play in our favor as they will not suspect our real offensive attacks.

Our themes are different, but both sides are employing propaganda as a "weapon." We are both engaging in psychological warfare. The problem is, this kind of warfare only works when morale is low. Ours is not.

Steadfast and Loyal,
Uncle Jim

Beth Rieman is in Delaware, Ohio

September 15, 2018 at 12:00 pm • Delaware, OH

I thought I would share something I found because I thought it was fascinating. This is a German newspaper from WWII. It has a picture of a ship that was used to carry vehicles, tanks, cargo, etc., on D-Day, designed to allow everything to be unloaded directly on shore, without piers or ports. The caption of the picture is telling readers that this Allied carrier was unloading onto a barge on D-Day and that the barge was completely destroyed by German artillery fire. The headline is purposely fabricated to make people think that the Germans did a lot of damage on D-Day, when in fact, nothing in this picture was blown up or harmed in any way (Uncle Jim was on that ship and is mentioned in the typed note).

I'm not as surprised by the propaganda, though, as I am surprised to read HOW the picture came to be published in German newspapers. Apparently, an American journalist took the picture and sent the film to England with a CARRIER PIGEON! The pigeon went the wrong direction and flew all the way to Germany, falling exhausted into a German soldier's hands. The Germans must have developed the film and decided to use the picture in their own way, to encourage their citizens to support their war efforts and to make them believe they were winning the war.

Forgive me if I am late to the game, but I had not realized carrier pigeons were used past medieval times! Crazy!

170 | ELIZABETH RIEMAN

German newspaper propaganda

JIM

NOVEMBER 14, 1944

Dear Rose,

Well, our superiors were wrong about the war being over before Christmas, and we are paying the price for their decision to not bring in winter supplies. It is cold, damp, and miserable here. The feelings of triumph I had a month ago are fading to feelings of discouragement as I watch our men become distressed by the misery of our situation.

No amount of training can prepare you for the terrible things you see and the brutal things you do when you are on the frontlines. Your eyes are bombarded with visuals that burn into your brain and stay there: a helmet on the ground with a soldier's scalp inside, a man still alive but with his legs blown off, the fear in the enemy's eyes as you kill him. However, after that first battle, you get hardened to it, and it does not affect you in the same way. You have to become hardened or you will lose your mind. What once haunted you is now something that doesn't even register. You become a killing machine and you are numb to the aftermath. It's a conundrum though, because once you are hardened, and you have time to really think about it, you start to worry about the fact that you have become desensitized to the grotesque aspects of war. I'm not sure human beings are wired to experience the psychological distress we endure.

At our most recent engagement, we were joined by reinforcements from another division, one which had been rotating soldiers in and out of rest periods and had sent groups back to England for longer breaks. Trying to establish rapport with his new comrades, one of the incoming sergeants joked with a group in our regiment and said, "The coffee at our last camp was miserable. I said to my men, 'If you can survive the coffee, you can survive the war!'" He did not get the response he expected; our soldiers did not laugh; they stared at him, expressionless. What that sergeant did not know is that the 4th Infantry Division has been in contact with the enemy for almost two-hundred consecutive days and no one has been sent to England for rest.

The daily life of an infantryman in our division is grim right now. Our men have eaten frozen rations because we were unable to warm them, have used snow to make the powdered drinks from our packs because our water was frozen, have slept on rocks instead of the ground because rocks are at least relatively dry, and have lived under relentless artillery fire, unable to move for long periods of time.

You don't even consider how taking care of the most basic of needs is dangerous on the battlefield. Should a man need to relieve himself, he has to consider the fact that emerging from his trench means putting a target on his back. There is no worry of modesty, only worry of the shellings or of a German sniper's aim. If he can, he crawls out, takes down his drawers and exposes his skin to the bitter cold. He takes care of business as quickly as possible (fearful the entire time) and runs back to his hole, dressing himself along the way. He cannot even afford to pull up his pants until he reaches his slit trench, for that is a gamble with his life; those extra few seconds, redressing while he is out of the trench, expose him to enemy attack.

Bathing is an unheard of luxury and many men have not showered in six months. We wear dirty clothes that are grimy from constant wear, filthy from so much combat, and, quite honestly, the changing of underwear is something that happens at home, not at war. We are wearing the same overcoats now as we did in England and they are heavy, bulky coats that make it difficult to move, and they are even worse when wet. Which is all the time.

Infantrymen quickly learn to live with only the basic necessities. They rid themselves of personal possessions because they have to carry everything and their packs are already heavy, weighing around sixty pounds. Their clothing alone weighs another twenty pounds. And their rifles weigh around ten pounds. Possessions beyond this must be considered essential to be added to their pack which are carried through all kinds of weather and terrain, for hours on end.

Dry socks are a soldier's most important possession. The army issued shoes are not good in these weather conditions and are in a constant state of wetness, as are in turn, socks. Wet socks mean blisters and trench foot. Blisters mean terrible discomfort for a soldier who is constantly moving. Trench foot means the infirmary. So, soldiers have learned to keep as many pairs of socks stuffed on their person as they can. They rotate socks by removing their wet pair and washing them out in the snow. They then retrieve a dry pair from under their helmet, inside a sleeve, in a pocket, or from wherever they have them stuffed. The wet pair that has just been washed in the snow is then placed in the spot from which the dry pair came in order to be used in a future rotation.

On the frontline, even darkness does not bring relief. Because of our close proximity to the enemy and a need to remain hidden, on the frontline we are not allowed to smoke cigarettes or start fires by which to heat rations or get warm. We have to remain alert so we sit in slit-trenches, back to back with a buddy, which allows the pair to have a 360-degree view at all times. Sometimes, we are not sure when we will be granted an hour or more of sleep. Enlisted men also have to rotate in and out of listening posts, defensive posts, and night-watch shifts.

Miserable weather, bitter cold, lack of sleep, constant fear, poor nutrition, wet socks — there is never a break from any of this. So, soldiers were not sympathetic when they heard that sergeant say, "The coffee at our last camp was miserable. I said to my men, 'If you can survive the coffee, you can survive the war!'" You must forgive them, Sergeant, but coffee, even the worst tasting coffee, is an everyday comfort our men would welcome on the frontlines.

Steadfast and Loyal,
Uncle Jim

DECEMBER 5, 1944

Dear Rose,

I apologize for the length of time between letters. What I have to describe to you will make you understand the delay. The Hürtgen Forest was the most horrendous fighting situation I have ever been in, something we could not have imagined when preparing for this war. It baffles me that the 4th Infantry Division was sent there to fight for the past month, because, as you remember, during my brief time with the 9th Infantry division, there had already been attacks planned there, and that fighting had proven unproductive and costly. This past month, with the 4th Infantry Division, was pure Hell just as it had been for those who fought there before us.

Our assignment was to breakthrough and capture objectives beyond the forest, but we had to first push through a dense, wooded area, twenty miles long, ten miles deep, with trees up to one hundred feet high. You will have never seen an area with woods so thick. The forest itself became our objective because it was practically impenetrable. There were deep gorges, high swampy meadows, and dense undergrowth. Constant rain had made the ground a muddy disaster and vehicles could not pass without getting stuck. That same rain flooded the streams and deteriorated the roads. The weather made visibility difficult and this, combined with the closely packed trees, meant air support was not possible. The forest's canopy blocked most of the sunlight, so the woods were dark and ominous, a perfect metaphor for the way we felt.

The weather was unbearable: heavy rain, snow, near freezing temperatures at times. The brief breaks in rain and snow were not long enough to dry out the ground. This created a sea of mud, causing a transport problem as vehicles could not get through. Supplies, therefore, had to be brought in on foot, and this could not happen quickly enough because men were often up to their knees in mud. The men who brought the water, rations, and supplies slugged under constant threat of the enemy who could materialize at any moment, hidden in defensive areas in their built-in strong points, their positions dug in and well-guarded by wire, minefields, and small arms fire.

The Germans had six years to prepare the forest for their defense. They built log bunkers. They covered the forest floor with landmines. They pruned the trees to create paths for interlocking gunfire that would kill our approaching troops. They built pillboxes in outpost locations that provided them with superb views of the forest, while we were afforded no views at all. And they used all of this to their benefit, annihilating entire groups of men daily.

Fighting was brutal. By the time our regiment arrived, we were already down one regiment because the 12th had already lost 1,600 men. The trees were very dense with only infrequent, small areas of open ground. We had some room to crawl at the base of the trees, but we were met with incessant shelling. The hills were mined so we had to avoid them completely and, in the small clearings, we tried to throw logs to trigger the mines we were likely to step on every 10 paces or so. We could not detect the enemy more than five yards away, yet the enemy could see us from their outposts and would fire at every movement, their dug in machine guns set up to spray in interlocking fire. They had excellent positions protected by three layers of barbed-wire, mortar barrages, small arms fire, and mines, and they only became visible when they came out of hiding during counterattacks. The rest of the time, we were unsure of their locations.

The slightest movement we made forward meant stopping almost immediately to take cover. Taking cover meant digging new trenches and cutting logs to place over top. If we didn't cover the tops of the trenches, we risked death from tree bursts when the enemy purposely fired into the trees so that fatal fragments of bark would come showering down on us in our trenches. The trenches filled with inches of icy water in which men were expected to fight, eat, sleep, and even relieve themselves. Because they would be immediately fired upon, it was often impossible to leave the trenches to "take care of business," which meant filling the watery puddles with urine and depositing bodily waste in empty ration cans.

Darkness comes quickly this time of year, so soldiers would have to hunker down in those wet, cold trenches and stay there for long hours. The constant wetness led to a great number of trench foot cases where men's feet became infected which caused calloused layers of tissue on their feet to die and fall off. Men then had to be removed from battle because, if not treated, trench foot could lead to amputation and even death. Men quickly lost any sense of shame, removing socks from the bodies of dead soldiers to procure as their own in order to avoid this fate. The number of men with trench foot added to the large number of casualties and platoons were quickly becoming depleted. The enemy, on the other hand, brought in reinforcements daily and moved in masses at night so they could attack us early in the morning.

Because armor support was impossible through the mud and through the mines, because air support was impossible with poor visibility, the fight became a direct ground assault. We moved forward, one tree at a time. This made a gain of 600 yards take an entire day. It would take 4-5 days to move one mile. We moved, at this slow pace, among bodies rotting on the forest floor, through trees that held blown body parts in their branches, and past wild dogs feeding on corpses. We fought every day and pushed through complete exhaustion without losing cohesion. This is not an easy feat considering this claustrophobic, miserable, cold hell was also psychologically exhausting. Our fighting spirit and sense of duty drove us on where further advance seemed impossible.

Lt. Colonel George Mabry is a perfect example of this fighting spirit. Like so often was the case for anyone fighting in the Hürtgen, he and his men were halted when they came to an enemy minefield covered by heavy fire. He was tired of the endless hindrances in the forest, and, with a strong sense of duty, entered the minefield alone. Mabry personally dug some of the mines out of the field with a trench knife, cut through wire and disabled explosives, and made safe passage through the field for his men. Then, going ahead of his men alone, he charged and captured three enemy foxholes with his bayonet. Moving ahead again, Mabry captured three enemy bunkers, killing nine Germans in hand-to-hand combat with the butt of his rifle and his bayonet. Adrenaline rushing, he kept moving forward and charged the main bunker, killing six more Germans with his bayonet! Such heroic bravery opened an approach for Allied forces.

Still, no momentum could be achieved because any progress Mabry's unit and others made in the forest was held off while we waited for supplies or for other battalions who were delayed by similar obstacles. It became a vicious cycle of dealing with weather, terrain, and supply issues. Sometimes we couldn't even determine our location in order to communicate between regiments, the deep woods nondescript and never-ending. Mounting casualties diminished our lines, supplies were not coming in, communication was confused, and we were barely covering any ground each day.

For the average infantry foot slogger, when he peered out of his trench, his disgust was profound. His body revolted at the thought of the increasing pace of the campaign and tenacity of the enemy. His mind was sick from the sight and smell of blood and death mingled with the soaked earth about him. The situation in the forest went from bad to worse to abysmal. Men, who at the start of the war wanted nothing more than to survive the war alive and unharmed, started to realize that a wound meant a ticket home and that death meant peace.

Finally, after weeks of this claustrophobic misery, we were withdrawn and refitted for the next objective. We moved on without any celebration because there was no glory in what we had just experienced, nothing to celebrate after a month spent in complete agony. I don't think there is any way to physically or mentally prepare for the cold Hell we faced in the Hürtgen Forest. It was a death factory.

Steadfast and Loyal,
Uncle Jim

UNPACKING YESTERDAY | 179

Newspaper clipping, found in Uncle Jim's scrapbook

Beth Rieman is in Delaware, Ohio
June 1, 2019 at 12:00 pm • Delaware, OH

The Ivy House, Hemingway Room

Upon careful consideration, checking finances, and weighing the options, it has been decided that only one of us will travel to France to donate the cane, taking advantage of the town's generosity in paying for a plane ticket. I am the lucky one who will travel this summer to do so. I will Facetime with my mom while I am there and take lots of pictures and videos so that she can experience it virtually, but I do wish she would come with me. It will be a once-in-a-lifetime experience, I know. I am excited, nervous, and emotional, all at the same time.

I found this B&B, which is a half mile walk to the museum where the cane will be donated. It is named "The Ivy House," in honor of the 4th Infantry Division which makes it sentimental to me since this is the same division in which Teddy Roosevelt, Jr. and Uncle Jim were active. This B&B was once occupied by German soldiers manning the bunkers of the Atlantic Wall coastal defenses during D-Day so it was part of history as well. The rooms are named "Roosevelt" (for Teddy Roosevelt, Jr), "Barton" (for Raymond O Barton, commander of the 4th Infantry Division), and "Hemingway" (because Hemingway was embedded with the 4th Infantry Division during WWII). Seems fated, doesn't it? Unfortunately, "Hemingway" is the smallest of the three and where I will be staying (Roosevelt would have been PERFECT), but I feel like Roosevelt and Barton are there to make it feel "right."

JIM

DECEMBER 9, 1944

Dear Rose,

Now that we finally moved out of the Hürtgen Forest, our division needs some rest. We are a very tired, depleted unit. It is time for us to reorganize, receive replacements, and train, so we have been assigned to an area that is much less active. It will be nice to be away from frontline combat for a bit as we try to put the past month behind us. We have fought for 199 days straight without rest.

Some good news: I was promoted in rank from Colonel to Brigadier General. For this to happen, my files and efficiency reports had to be carefully studied, letters from superiors reviewed, and a recommendation then was submitted to the President of the United States who had to make the nomination official. Then the nomination moved to the Senate where it was approved. This promotion is an honor, one that carries with it more responsibility and one that holds me to a higher standard.

I am sure my previous position as chief of staff, and current position as Assistant Divison Commander under Genera Barton was key in accelerating my promotion. These positions hold more weight than a colonel who sits behind a desk and I am fortunate that Barton trusted me to be his right-hand man. Additionally, having served as commander of the

8th Infantry Regiment must have helped with my promotion, showing my record as a leader and showing my worth as a soldier. Barton once said of me, to Ernie Pyle, "If anything, he is too bold. If he is not careful, he's liable to get clipped." That made me proud, because I want to be seen as a soldier first. I don't want to be a figurehead, one of those ranking officers who receive medals for their leadership without stepping foot on the battlefield. I refuse to push orders on my men without being part of the action. I will not be an armchair Brigadier General. Like Ted, I want to lead from the front.

This evening, as I traded my eagle for my star, I was filled with so much pride. I thought about all that came before this day, and all the great men in the Army who have mentored me and believed in me. I am so happy that Tubby did the honors of pinning on the star, but I sure wish Ted could have been here to see it. I did make sure that the cane was there for the ceremony, but my dear friend was only there in spirit. Another celebratory moment with a bittersweet undercurrent.

Steadfast and Loyal,
Uncle Jim

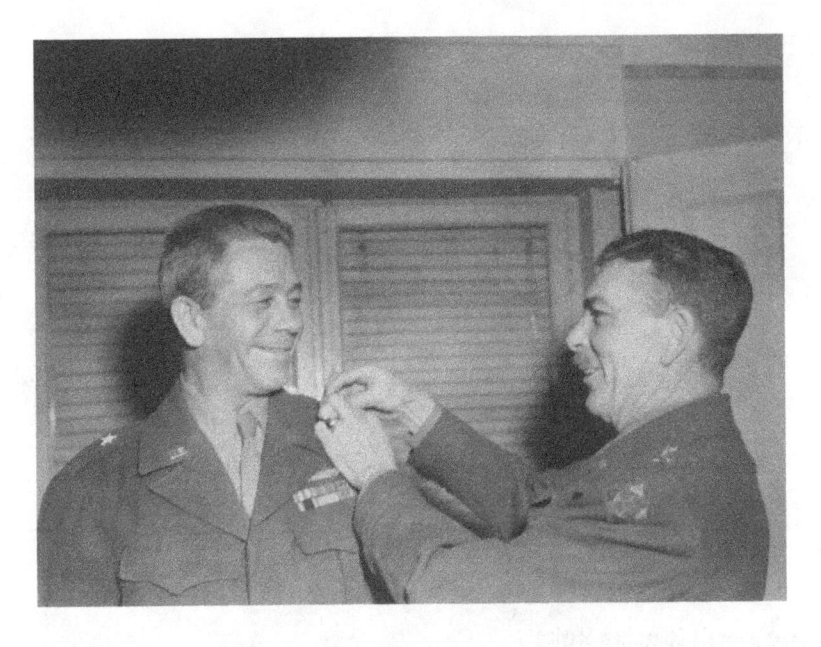

*Uncle Jim, receiving his Brigadier General star, Barton doing the honors.
(picture found among Uncle Jim's mementos)*

Various newspaper clippings announcing James S. Rodwell's promotion to Brigadier General

DECEMBER 26, 1944

Dear Rose,

I am sorry for the long delay since my last letter, but I think after reading this, you will understand why I was unable to write. After a month of complete Hell in the Hürtgen Forest, after our division suffered over 5,000 battle casualties and another 2,500 casualties to trench foot or exposure, after fighting without rest for 199 days straight, you will remember that our division was relieved and moved to a new area along the line, near Luxembourg. You will also remember that, in addition to the hellish fighting in the forest, our division had consistently engaged with the enemy since we landed in France on June 6. So, as soon as we were into the new area, we started a rotation line in order to allow men a few hours in Luxembourg City for rest, food, and beer. Others were given passes to Paris or Belgium for longer periods of rest.

Some replacements were brought in, but we were still operating with almost six hundred less men as a whole and, for infantry, that number was the worst. Our equipment was in bad shape after six months of constant use, and several tanks broke down on the way to Luxembourg. The 70th Tank Battalion, attached to our division, had only 11 tanks in operational condition (of their 54). Still, we felt like Luxembourg would be a welcome break from the cold, wet woods, and we knew we would not be having much contact with the enemy in this area, so the fact that we were short men was not a large concern. Furthermore, of the remaining troops, the men who set up in defensive positions in surrounding villages were at least warmer and drier indoors. The positions outside the villages were certainly not as warm and dry, but we were sure that this part of the map did not contain any tactical or strategic objectives so we did not expect there to be a lot of enemy contact. It would be a welcome rest for us, albeit cold.

What we didn't know was that Hitler had planned differently. While fewer Allied troops were deployed to our positions, Hitler planned a massive move into our lightly defended area. We learned later, from some of our prisoners, that our code-breakers did not pick up any warnings because the Germans had kept the offensive move a secret by insisting on a blackout of all radio communication regarding the planning. They told us that the Germans had excellent intelligence and knew our positions and our strength. They knew we had lost a lot of men and that our replacements were inexperienced. Hitler also formed a task force of English-speaking German soldiers who disguised themselves as Americans. They wore stolen Army uniforms, drove captured American jeeps, and carried American weapons. They posed as Americans and came behind our lines. They switched road signs to confuse movement, spread rumors among troops to cover-up plans, took out bridges, and cut communication lines.

Then, on December 16, we were surprised at all sectors. We were pounded by the enemy, so much that the ground shook. General Barton was alerted to enemy movement and sent a message, but wire communication had been severed and our radios malfunctioned. Therefore, our outposts were caught off guard and Barton's message was not received until well after the surprise attack began. One command post was left open to attack and had to hastily assemble a defense using cooks, MPs, and one tank. It was pure chaos and confusion. Our regiments, all in retrograde movement, expecting to see no action, were now being attacked! On top of that, everyone was isolated, not knowing the full scope of what was occurring, since we could not communicate with each other. With the radios that were actually working, we had very limited communication because the terrain outside the village sectors was rugged and interfered with frequencies. Without adequate communication, the 4th Infantry Division headquarters had no clear idea of the magnitude of the onslaught. We were facing a fully forced enemy, without enough men, and without communication with HQ.

We had three areas on which to concentrate our defense: a gorge and the wooded bluff above it that had very similar terrain to the Hürtgen Forest, an area with a network of roads that led to valuable supplies and command/communication centers, and a town that needed cleared of resistance. Each of the three areas were difficult to defend, especially with a battle-worn, understrength division that was not operating with sufficient means of communication.

In the gorge, we were fighting on terrain that became an additional obstacle, another enemy for us to overcome. There were steep, canyon like cliffs with massive crevasses full of huge boulders and rushing streams at their bases. This was all in a thick area of forest, where we found ourselves in wooded, rocky, snow covered mountains, called the Schnee Eifel. The openings to the gorges that cut through the forest were very narrow and tanks had to travel single-file through, with only the lead tank being able to fire. When the lead tank was hit, it took a long time to maneuver the remaining tanks around. So, every yard gained was gradual and was met by bazooka, mortar fire, and bullets from the enemy who was in hidden positions.

In the areas outside the gorge, the previous days' weather had turned the countryside to mud. The main roads were impassable by tanks, so armored support could only travel on alternate roads that were extremely narrow and unstable. This hurt us, but it hurt the enemy more. Our infantry was outnumbered by the Germans, but General Barton quickly gave orders that artillery was not to move rearward. Therefore, our tanks added power against the enemy's infantry who were fighting without heavy weapon support and found themselves halted on the roads when they came to bridges that had been destroyed. They couldn't bring their tanks into position to support their infantry and fight against us, tank to tank. Therefore, though outnumbered, our infantry, in combination with our forward positioned tanks, presented a strong defense.

In our third area of defense (the town), our men faced a three-hour barrage and a house to house assault following the initial surprise attack. While the main strength of our division had been placed in nearby villages prior to the surprise attack, the towns were only manned by small companies of men. Worse, the 4th Infantry Division only had one reserve battalion assigned to us because this was supposed to be a period of rest, and that reserve battalion was set to move with a four-hour notice. At this point, they were certainly put on notice, but they would not arrive quickly and four hours was a long time to wait. The troops of men who had been sent to France for rest were ordered up, but would not be in Luxembourg quickly. Other reserves were also called, but it would take time for us to receive reinforcements. The town was encircled by the enemy with only 60 men between the enemy and the post and with no back up arriving to support.

We held the Germans off that first day, despite the surprise attack, but knew we would have to fight them still the next day, with our line even more depleted than before and with our numbers still considerably less than the enemy's. We had to hold out for support to arrive. We had to continue to fight with deficits mounting.

The next day's weather was foggy and cold. We could not get air support because the weather kept them grounded. We had to hold a thin line against an enemy that was bringing in new soldiers sooner than our reinforcements could arrive. Just beyond our division's positions, with the Germans attacking this same way along the entire defensive front, the center of the Allied line suffered and the enemy advanced. Our Allied front that stretched 75 miles along the Ardennes Forest had now been pushed back at the center, creating a bulge in the middle of a previously taut line.

Our division continued to engage in savage fighting, on the left/southern flank of the line, while the Germans tried to dislodge us and break through. We were facing dire consequences. We used our cooks, drivers, and mess personnel and moved them to the line to help hold it. We struggled, but we did it! We were stretched across a thirty-five mile section, with tired and depleted companies every few miles, but we held our section of the front. We defended our position, less in number, but mightier in spirit!

Finally, our division's reinforcements and men from reserves arrived at midnight on the 18th, but our communication was still terrible. Failures in communication not only caused confusion, but also deaths. In the town of Osweiler, American soldiers attacked another American battalion as it was entering the town, thinking they were German soldiers since there was no communication to alert of their arrival. In another area, an entire company was missing and communication reports first had the company as surrounded by the enemy, second quickly correcting that report to say they were actually leaving the town, and third receiving another report that the company was being forced to surrender; communication consisted of a constant back-and-forth exchange with conflicting information. A tank battalion had to be sent in to locate that company and the situation ended with Allied officers, enlisted men, and a command post being captured by the enemy. All because of inadequate communication.

Fortunately, our soldiers were also creating chaos and havoc among the Germans. By the third day of fighting, we had destroyed bridges at critical river crossings, knocked out transportation and supply areas, and had moved to plug the gaps in our lines. We were not the only side with communication issues; German communication was a complete failure as well and prisoners told us that their army was confused and uninformed of battalion locations. Germans were also worried about their supplies and were running out of gasoline and ammo. Barton's decision to deny rear movement of our tanks and artillery put us in a good position in all three of the areas we were concentrated. In the area of the gorge, while one portion was under extremely heavy shellfire, tanks cut their engines to roll down the lower slope and surprised the enemy, clearing Germans from the area and seizing high ground.

Over the next few days, even in moments where the enemy was regrouping to defensive positions, we encountered fighting. We worked to reposition and were met by roadblocks that needed to be cleared, burning buildings, and pockets of resistance. We knew we had to hold the Germans off until reinforcements from other divisions could be assembled for counterattacks. We knew we had to hold our flank and defend an area three times the size of what was typical in any other situation. We had no choice because we could not let them make the center bulge any bigger (already 50 miles wide and 70 miles deep) and we could not let them penetrate the flanks at all. So, we held the left flank with all our might.

As the days moved forward, the weather started to clear, which allowed for air support. We were able to withdraw our advance detachments and bring the German attack on our flank to a halt. We jammed their advance and successfully defended our positions. In the towns close to the Sauer River, we successfully defended critical supply areas. We had fought for an entire month in the forest and we were exhausted, but the momentum from this successful defense kept us focused until we could be relieved. We were on an adrenaline high. In one of the towns, an explosion launched a toilet and sink from the upper story of a building, both landing on the deck of one of our tanks. Our men, without missing a beat, laughed at the surprise gifts and one soldier shouted, "What? You won't also send us a shower?!"

Over the course of ten days, we successfully defended the towns and the supplies that were beyond, blocked the roads from enemy advance, and thwarted the enemy's attempted penetration of our left flank. What we are now calling "The Battle of the Bulge" was far from over, but our part in holding the line until the rest of the Allied Army could mount a counterattack was complete. Our quick, strategic decisions had overcome a surprise attack that could have destroyed our entire division.

I still feel excited about how we brought the attack to a halt and held a thin, weak line against the enemy. They surprised us, but they couldn't defeat us. With men who were steadfast, we won a fierce, strategic battle. I am proud to be part of this division and I wish Ted had been here. As always, his cane was here in his place.

Steadfast and Loyal,
Uncle Jim

4th Inf. Div.

Luxembourg Saved By Stand of 4th

WITH FOURTH INF. DIV.—The stand of the Fourth Inf. Div from Dec. 16 to 26 "saved the city of Luxembourg." Lt. Gen. George S. Patton, Jr., wrote in a letter of commendation to Maj. Gen Raymond D Barton, division CG.

The 12th Inf. Regt and two other regiments of the Fourth were spread over a wide front when the big German offensive started.

"The Fourth Division's fight in the Hurtgen Forest was an epic of stark infantry combat," said Gen. Patton, "but in my opinion, its more recent fight—when the division halted the left shoulder of the German thrust and saved the city of Luxembourg—is the most outstanding accomplishment of the Fourth Div."

Newspaper clipping found in Uncle Jim's scrapbook

DECEMBER 25, 1944

Dear Rose,

Merry Christmas, Rose. This letter will be arriving late because mail is being curtailed even as I write this. By the time you receive this letter, Christmas will have passed, but right now it is Christmas evening. The worst of our fighting is over, the surprise attack by the enemy has been thwarted. The weather finally cleared, making air support possible, but there are still men on the battlefield fighting the final stubborn pockets of resistance. Our division experienced some fighting yesterday, but mainly in the morning. Since then, our division's regiments have moved to new positions in new sectors, and our 8th Infantry Regiment is on the outpost line (which means we are farther away from the fighting, not on the frontline). We have spent the past few days actively patrolling with very little resistance from the enemy, readjusting our positions, and repairing/cleaning our equipment.

Tonight, we celebrated Christmas the best we could. We topped a short evergreen and made a little Christmas tree for our table. The Army gave us a bit of Christmas dinner, and we were grateful to have something other than a K ration. Some wine had been looted from a nearby village and we made a simple toast: for our lives and for our freedoms. Ted's presence was felt, as always, because his cane was there, and I privately made a toast to him as well. How I wish he could be with us. The Army chaplain read from the Bible and we sang as many Christmas songs as we knew. There were no twinkling lights, no stockings by the fire, and no gifts, but for a few hours, we were able to share a bit of cheer.

It is bitter cold still, with a heavy frost, but it is dry for now. My thoughts turn to the troops who will spend this holiday on the battlefield. This evening, they will take turns with each other, hoping to catch an hour or two of restful sleep. They will dream of warmth, and home,

196 | ELIZABETH RIEMAN

and Christmases past. They will hope for a different kind of Christmas in the future; they will hope for any Christmas in the future — any Christmas where they are alive and away from this war.

Steadfast and Loyal,
Uncle Jim

Found among Uncle Jim's mementos. The 4th Infantry Division crossed the Siegrfried Line twice in the same sector during WWII — once in September 1944 and again in February 1945. Troops commented about occupying in February the same foxholes they had dug in September.

DECEMBER 27, 1944

Dear Rose,

I am sad today as I say goodbye to General Barton. He called a meeting to let us know he was leaving the 4th Infantry Division for health reasons. He has been our commander since June of '42, and frankly, the best I have ever worked under. Major General Eddy spoke of Barton, "The pages you have written in the history of the 4th Infantry Division will surely be red-letter pages in the history of the United States Army. You battled on the beaches of Normandy on D-Day; you drove through the German line in the great July breakthrough at St. Lo; you were the first into Paris in August; you swept across France and Belgium, reached the Siegfried Line, and were the first into Germany in September; you held at bay an entire German Corps in the Luxembourg area in December. During this remarkable campaign, your Division maintained always an efficiency and spirit which could come only from leadership in its highest sense."

I can't write it any better.

As you know, Tubby has been one of my closest friends on and off the battlefield, and though we will remain comrades, it is disheartening to recognize that he will not be leading us every day. I know that he does not want to leave us, but, after almost eight months of combat, he is in poor health with a duodenal ulcer. He deserves a rest; he needs a rest. He led our division to victory, battle after battle, and I could not feel more honored to have served with him and to call him my friend.

General Blakeley will assume command.

Steadfast and Loyal,
Uncle Jim

198 | ELIZABETH RIEMAN

Picture found among Uncle Jim's mementos, General Barton being sworn in, 1942, James Van Fleet on the left

JANUARY 22, 1945

Dear Rose,

January came rushing in with blizzards, freezing rain, and record low temperatures. It is so cold and icy that vehicles often become frozen to the ground overnight. Tanks slide on the roads. Canteens freeze. Weapons jam. We are mostly on the move, but when we have to stop and dig in, the ground is so frozen that we cannot dig trenches; we have to use grenades and explosives to blow holes in the ground. It is difficult to maintain supply routes due to the poor road conditions.

It is an understatement to say that weather has become a formidable adversary.

Today, enemy small arms fire was heavy from emplacements along the Siegfried Line and tanks were observed in various places. The 8th Infantry Regiment used our own supporting tanks and made good progress while also continuing to improve our defensive positions on the high ground facing the Our River. The 12th Infantry Regiment attacked and advanced, sometimes in the face of stiff resistance and other times against little opposition, capturing the town of Walsdorf. The 22nd Infantry Regiment maintained defenses, with some men moving to an assembly area in the vicinity of Haller.

We are tired, cold, and fighting the weather as much as we are battling the enemy, but we know a spring thaw is on the horizon. We also know that the enemy is handicapped on many levels. They are unable to resupply depleted military equipment because their factories have been destroyed. Casualties have claimed the majority of their soldiers, so they are fighting with drafted troops who are at the youngest and oldest ends of the spectrum. The enemy's impairments are aiding in our advance. We can push through, knowing that the winter weather will be over soon. Spring will surely usher in the end of the war in Europe.

Steadfast and Loyal,
Uncle Jim

Uncle Jim, January 1945

FEBRUARY 14, 1945

Dear Rose,

What a strange coincidence today...We broke through the Siegfried Line at the same point we broke through in September. That is to say, we broke through at the same sector, but we certainly did not break through with the same group of men. In September, we had not yet fought in the Hürtgen Forest or in the Battle of the Bulge. In September, we thought the war in Europe was coming to an end. We have lost so many great soldiers since then.

I know we are all feeling the effects of being engaged in combat for such a long period of time, with very little breaks. I am certainly feeling the strain. Battle brings on such strange dichotomies of emotions: fear and bravery, killing and remorse, homesickness and belonging, misery and purpose. Much of our experiences in battle are in direct conflict with what we have been taught our whole lives, such as the fact that killing is no longer forbidden, but actually required. However, the traumatizing experiences of frontline battle are masked by the adrenaline rush we feel when we are in direct combat. We are all homesick, wanting to return to our families, but we have also become close as brothers and we will miss each other when this is all over. These emotions seem to be in conflict with each other, but somehow, it all works to balance the negative and positive aspects of life in the Army. The terrible weather, rations, stress, lack of sleep, and constant uncertainty are balanced by the bonds we form with each other, the unity we experience as a nation, and the selfless sacrifice that inspires us to be brave. Yet, even with this balance, it is often hard to keep our minds strong when our bodies are so tired. We have to remember what we are fighting for and why we are here. And we have to lean on each other to keep moving forward. I feel I am tempting fate to write that the war is winding down, but it is just a matter of time now.

Steadfast and Loyal,
Uncle Jim

MARCH 10, 1945

Dear Rose,

We recently pushed to cross the Kyll River at which point I was assigned a special task force, named "Task Force Rhino." This consisted of infantry, field artillery, and the 70th Tank Battalion. We were to move ahead and take out pockets of resistance. Our men had been fighting for so long, seen so much action now, that we were feeling the effects of what had become a sound, tactical division and we were driven by that momentum. We were in full on pursuit of the retreating enemy. We drove through the rain and snow, mud and sludge, as the Germans fought back each step of the way. We encountered blown bridges and hastily erected roadblocks, barricades and resistance, but we were not stopped. Short fire fights ensued along the way, but the enemy never lasted more than a day. We were too much for them to handle.

Our task force crossed a river that other units had tried to cross previously and failed. That river may have thwarted other men, but we initiated the advance and kept going, no thought to what had come before us. Feeling the thrill of combat victory, our task force decided to make a mad dash for 24 hours and covered more than 20 miles. Can you imagine, infantry covering that kind of ground in just 24 hours? We were ready to end this thing and we were feeling strong, almost immortal.

In the darkness of night, we entered a town that was occupied by the enemy. At this point, we did not have the support of combat support troops — it was just this group of men with me leading them on foot through the town. We knew we had no back up to help us, we knew we had targets on our backs, but we were determined, and I made sure my men remained brave and focused and alert. Along the way, we eliminated every point of resistance and surmounted every obstacle the Germans left for us.

We then cleared and captured Honerath, Rodder, Adenau and Reifferscheid, pushing the retreating Germans even further away, watching them run with their tails between their legs. I was proud to turn Adenau over to Major General Middleton because he was an officer with the 4th Infantry Division in the last war and had occupied the same town 27 years ago. That's right — twice the Americans took that town!

We collected 1500 prisoners, and only were down two casualties, four wounded, and one light tank. We are feeling the excitement of victory right now. I'm telling you, Rose, the Nazis are done for and I can't imagine this war lasting much longer.

Steadfast and loyal,
Uncle Jim

> Brigadier General JAMES S RODWELL, 09663, United States Army, 4th Infantry Division, United States Army. JAMES S RODWELL, 09663, Brigadier General, United States Army, 4th Infantry Division, while a member of the armed forces of the United States distinguished himself by extraordinary heroism in connection with military operations against an armed enemy in the vicinity of ADENAU and RIFFERSHEID, GERMANY, 8 and 9 March 1945. A task force under the leadership of General RODWELL initiated an advance, crossing a river which had thwarted similar previous attempts, and penetrated swiftly and deeply into enemy territory. The force, animated by his vigorous leadership, eliminated each enemy point of resistance and deftly surmounted each obstacle which the retreating Germans had left in their wake. He personally and on foot led his command group through an enemy occupied town at night while devoid of any support of assistance from combat troops. General RODWELL'S outstanding personal courage and aggressive leadership are in accord with the highest military traditions.

> By command of General PATTON:
>
> OFFICIAL
>
> HOBART R. GAY,
> Major General, U. S. Army,
> Chief of Staff.
>
> R. E. CUMMINGS,
> Colonel, Adjutant General's Department,
> Adjutant General.
>
> DISTRIBUTION:
> "A" "B" "J"
> 3 - TAG (Dec & Awards Br)   2 - CG 12th A Gp (G-1 Sec - 1)
> 4 - CG ETO US Army (AG Opns Div - 2)   (CG 37th MRU - 1)
>   (Awards & Doc Br, AG Mil Pers Div - 2) 9 - G-1, this Hq
>
> R-E-S-T-R-I-C-T-E-D

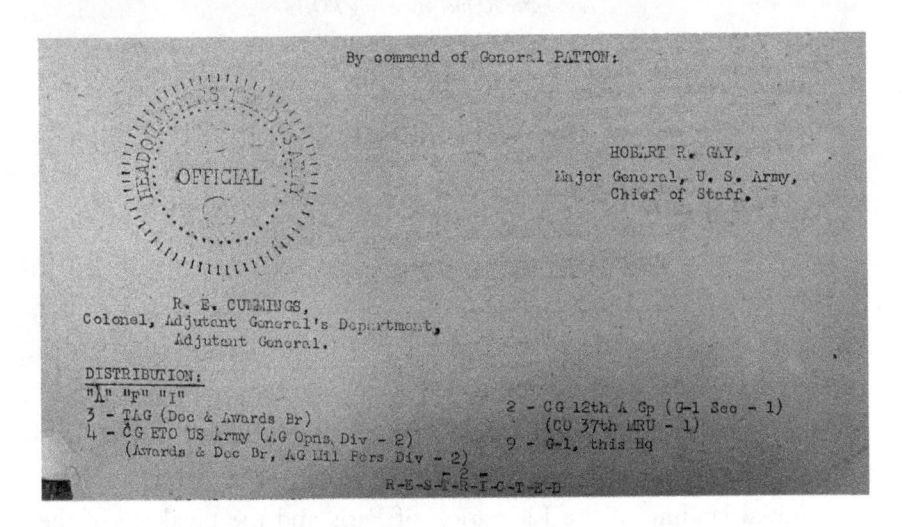

Official record, presentation of Distinguished Service Cross to Brigadier General James S. Rodwell for his leadership of a special task force in the advance to capture Adeanau and Reifferscheid (additional names removed for privacy)

Task Force Rhino, processing POWs

MARCH 16, 1945

Dear Rose,

Today our 8th Infantry Regiment received 1500 Presidential Unit Citation Badges to distribute among our men. Additionally, I was awarded the Legion of Honor, which is the highest award for valor in France, given for "extraordinary military bravery in times of war." This was awarded to encompass service during the Normandy Invasion: from our initial landing to the Liberation of Paris and the breaking of the Siegfried Line. I was also awarded the Croix de Guerre avec Palme, which is given to "individuals who distinguish themselves by acts of heroism involving combat with enemy forces." I am very proud to be recognized by Charles De Gaulle and the Republic of France, along with Barton, Blakely, Chance, Lanham, Luckett, Marr, and Reeder, who I count among my closest friends. However, I also know that I am not a hero. The enlisted infantrymen in my regiment are to be commended, and they are some of the last to receive the glory. They are the men who face danger, day in and day out. They are constantly in combat under the worst conditions and they don't get to remove to a command post position at any point. They are the backbone of the military and I am proud to be among them. I know they are the main force behind any awards I receive. And the men who gave their lives in this campaign — the men who sacrificed so that others could be free — they are the true heroes. I am humbled by the thought of the men who will posthumously receive awards, unable to be in the presence of their loved ones to celebrate their commendations.

Steadfast and Loyal,
Uncle Jim

Rio Grande City Officer Honored

MISSION — Brig. Gen. James S. Rodwell of Rio Grande City, assistant Divisional Commander of the 4th Infantry Division, has been awarded the Order of Chevalier of the Legion of Honor and the Croix De Guerre with Palm by the Provisional Government of the Republic of France, a dispatch this week from the Seventh Army in Germany revealed.

General Rodwell was a general staff officer with the Seventh when it stormed ashore at Hough on D-Day in Normandy and during the Normany breakthrough, the liberation of Paris, and the campaign during the breaking of the Seigfried Line. He was regimental commander of the first of the Division's regiments to receive a Presidential Citation.

In citation accompanying the awards from the Republic of France, General Rodwell was commended for "excepitonal services rendered in the course of operations of the liberation of France." It was signed by Gen. Charles De Gaulle, president of the French Provisional Government, and is one of the highest military awards made by the Republic of France.

General Rodwell, a former officer at Fort Ringgold, Rio Grande City, had previously received the Bronze Star, the Silver Star, and the Oak Leaf Cluster to the latter. His wife is the former Miss Pauline Drummond of Mission and Rio Grande City. Since he went overseas, she has been at home in the latter city where she and General Rodwell own a half-interest in the Hotel Ringgold.

A private in World War I, General Rodwell was commissioned a second lieutenant in the Cavalry in 1917. He continued to advance and to receive advanced training in Army schools during the peace years. Te was assigned to the General Staff Corps in 1940 and last November was promoted to his present rank.

Newspaper clipping, found in Uncle Jim's scrapbook

March 16, 1945- Uncle Jim, wearing the Legion of Honor, the evening it was awarded (found among Uncle Jim's mementos)

APRIL 4, 1945

Dear Rose,

We are deep into Germany now and, honestly, we are just waiting on a surrender. We still encounter resistance and light combat. I am not sure what the Germans think is going to happen now, what hopes they have of defeating our Allied forces.

Last night, the command post of our 8th Infantry Regiment was raided. About two dozen enemy soldiers snuck in with bazookas and grenades. They destroyed several of our vehicles (at least a dozen) and killed one soldier. What is the point in all of this? They certainly did not enter our post thinking they would win a hand-to-hand fight. They didn't stay to face us because their whole plan was cowardly; they just wanted to create confusion and chaos. I don't see the benefit of that. Are they symbolically spitting on us before they retreat?

Steadfast and Loyal,
Uncle Jim

APRIL 20, 1945

Dear Rose,

I have a rather funny story to relay to you. While temporarily located in a town in Germany, soldiers in our first battalion were approached by a German woman who asked that the Americans take over her supply of liquor. Her husband was a liquor dealer and their basement was full of many kinds of liquor in abundant supply: gin, brandies, vermouth, cognac, wine, really anything you could imagine.

Well, it seems that, a few months ago, knowing we were quickly advancing toward their town, her husband had rounded up Russian prisoners and had them seal the liquor supply in with cement, so that it would be hidden from Allied troops. What he hadn't considered, however, was that those same Russian prisoners who had worked to conceal the liquor, once liberated by our Allied troops, would remember what they had been forced to do and would wish to return to claim the liquor supply as their own. The wife had learned that liberated Russians were on their way to her home with axes and sledge hammers, and thinking of how poorly the Germans typically treated Russian prisoners, she was not only worried about the safety of the liquor supply. She felt that that neither the liquor, her home, nor her life would be spared, especially after the Russians consumed some of the supply. Therefore, the woman was seeking help from the very men from whom the supply was meant to be hidden in the first place.

We were quick to overlook the liquor dealer's original intent and the woman did not have to ask twice for our assistance. The battalion, seeing it as our duty to maintain order, allowed some men to guard the cellar where the liquor was stored. If need be, the plan was to confiscate the supply. Now, we really couldn't keep a constant rotation of men on guard, so it was decided that the best way to keep the liquor supply out of the Russians' possession would be to liquidate it. It was also decided that the best way to liquidate it would be to drink it. Therefore, the liquor was quickly packed up and taken away.

The German woman, seeing the liquor leaving her cellar, asked the lieutenant in charge of the detail to make sure the American government would pay for the supply. She even presented him with a bill of sale that amounted to an equivalent of $5,000. The lieutenant, being quick on his feet, agreed to her demands and even offered to personally write a receipt for the liquor. He wrote a receipt (in English of course) and handed it to the woman who was very pleased with herself and satisfied with the exchange. Little did she know, the receipt read, "This is to certify that the American Army has this day confiscated the liquor supply of this concern to the sum of five thousand dollars ($5,000), this sum to be deducted from the amount of money which the German Government owes the American Government from World War I."

I can just picture her waiting for the money to come, and I sure would like to be there when she realizes it never will.

Steadfast and Loyal,
Uncle Jim

APRIL 25, 1945

Dear Rose,

It has been almost a month since we crossed the Rhine and we continue in final pursuit of the enemy. For the past few days, I have led a task force in an advance that facilitated the further advance of a combat team as it drove the Germans back, surrounding them and forcing a surrender. At first, we were only hampered by numerous road blocks, cratered roads, and blown bridges, but then we encountered resistance. Our forward elements were bombed and strafed by a plane before we overcame resistance on the high ground southwest of Crailsheim. We had to work through the night to make the road to our advance passable and began attacking at first light, this assault leading to the clearing of Crailsheim.

The next day, we reached the edge of the woods north of Rindelbach where the enemy was engaged in a last-ditch effort to defend the town. We faced stubborn resistance of all types and were under continuous fire. We also faced obstacles presented by the terrain of the area. Our task force advanced steadily though, and by 0400, we passed through. Our forward elements continued south and engaged in a short-fire fight until the enemy retreated on bicycles.

Moving forward, we met strong resistance and we lost two tanks as well as some men. It took another ten hours to eliminate the enemy and we moved southeast, unopposed. However, once we reached the vicinity of Aalen, we were met by 500-600 enemy soldiers with small arms and bazookas. We moved through Aalen against strong delaying action for another three hours until the enemy was finally seen fleeing into the woods.

Road blocks, destroyed bridges, and craters forced us toward Wasseralfingen (north of Aalen) during the night. Reinforced by two companies of tanks, we surrounded the town, but it was a slow advance. We had to search all buildings because any enemies left behind would surely shoot to kill the combat team for whom we were clearing a path. The next morning, our advance was slowed even more by small arms, light artillery, and mortar fire as well as road blocks, cratered roads, and mines. We kept pushing through, though, and after four days, our task force was dissolved, having cleared the way for incoming troops. This allowed our division to then cover ground at a rapid pace. The city of Munich fell quickly and easily. We rounded up a lot of German prisoners and will continue to do so in the upcoming days.

It is over now. The war in Europe is over. Now we just wait for an inevitable surrender.

Steadfast and Loyal,
Uncle Jim

APRIL 30, 1945

Dear Rose,

A group of soldiers were on patrol and they came across an enclosed camp, surrounded by wooden posts and barbed wire. There were guard towers and a locked gate at the front of the enclosure. Soldiers shot off the lock and, when they stepped inside, they saw horrors worse than they had seen this entire campaign—worse than blood from fatal wounds, worse than blown off limbs, worse than patches of flesh strewn in fields. What was encountered beyond the gates will be a vision to haunt the rest of our lives.

The gates had been shot open, but the men inside the camp were so weak that they could barely shuffle their way to freedom. They were wearing striped pants and shirts with ragged scraps of cloth over their shoulders attempting to add warmth. Their cheeks were sunken and their eyes bulged from their sockets. Their shaven heads were covered with round caps and their bodies were not much more than skin on skeleton frames.

Their German guards had fled and left a pile of bodies to burn. The pile was a stack of about 400 bodies, and it was smoldering, having never been fully engulfed in flames. Most of the bodies were lifeless, but a few showed signs of slow struggle. The smell was something that cannot be described or forgotten.

The prisoners characterized their surroundings as a forced labor camp, a subcamp of the larger Dachau camp which has been liberated by two other American divisions, the 42nd Infantry Division and the 45th Infantry Division. This smaller subcamp of Dachau, the camp our division had entered, was one of several subcamps in the area. The prisoners had been moved here from larger camps in other countries just before those camps were liberated, and the Nazi guards who had been here were also previously stationed at those camps. Most of the men in this camp had already survived selection lines at other death camps and had seen their families die. By the time they were moved to this camp, they didn't have much reason left to hope.

Hitler originally "cleansed" his country of Jewish people, but he allowed the reintroduction of these laborers as a last, desperate attempt to win the war. The prisoners were brought here to construct underground facilities in which to manufacture jet fighters that could sweep the Allies. All above ground factories in Germany had been bombed by our Allied forces and Hitler needed to have subterranean factories with thick, reinforced roofs that could withstand air raids. He had designed and boasted about a faster, sleeker jet fighter that would end the war, with Germany as the victors. We found machines in the underground bunkers, but there were no planes yet.

The prisoners had been forced to build railroad embankments and haul bags of cement to speed along Hitler's plan. When they were unable to work, they were beaten. If the beatings were not "effective," and they still could not work, they were sent to larger camps to be gassed or sent to a different subcamp to die among prisoners infected with typhoid.

The men were also forced to build their own accommodations and this resulted in rows of pointed huts, partially underground, with earthen peaked roofs above ground. Down inside the huts, everything was cold and damp; the dirt floors were covered with hay on which to sleep and the hay was infested with fleas. There were some prisoners in these huts who were too weak to move towards the gates on their own; they were weak from starvation and from the severe beatings the Nazis inflicted. In the more recent months, the already scarce food rations allotted at camp had been reduced even more as Germans kept food for themselves in worried preparation for the end of the war.

When officers arrived and saw the horrors of the camp, they were enraged. Following the example from the stories we had heard of General Eisenhower when he visited the main Dachau camp soon after it was liberated, our officers and soldiers went into the village and rounded up as many male citizens as they could find and escorted them to the camp. They forced the towns' men to stand in silence and view the atrocities around them, atrocities in a camp not far from their home, impossible to believe they had not known. Then, they told those men to move the bodies. In pairs, men carried naked corpses to a designated area and a soldier followed them, rifle brandished. This continued until all the bodies were moved. Next, while under the rifles of our guards, the townsmen were forced to dig large graves until there was ample room in which to bury the victims. They then buried the victims and covered their graves without being permitted to utter a single word. When their work was completed, they were ushered from the camp under the glare of hateful, disgusted eyes. The people who denied the existence of the camp would not be allowed to deny it any longer and they would forever be haunted by the things they saw that day, just as our division would.

We were angry and appalled and devastated by the day's discovery, but we were also reminded of the reasons we had fought in this war. The war is coming to an end and Europe will be freed of an evil dictatorship.

Steadfast and Loyal,
Uncle Jim

Beth Rieman is in Delaware, Ohio
June 19, 2019 at 4:00 pm • Delaware, OH

John Hay, WWII veteran who helped hold the right flank during the Battle of the Bulge

Today was a good day. I was able to tell the story of the cane to two groups of senior citizens. At the first presentation, through tears, a woman told us that she was from France and felt so grateful for the men who came on D-Day. At the second presentation, a man shared that he was at the Battle of the Bulge holding the right flank against the German army while the 4th Infantry Division was holding the left flank. Another woman shared that her husband had been in WWII when he was 18 and that they were engaged while he was at war; she wishes she had saved their letters written back and forth during the war to leave as a legacy. These are just three of the stories I was able to hear, and walk away with in my heart, after sharing our family's discoveries. It was such a wonderful experience and I wish I could continue to meet people like this. Their lives are full of incredible stories that need to be heard. My heart is full.

JIM

MAY 5, 1945

Dear Rose,

Over the past week, we have been rounding up German soldiers by the hundreds and we have only encountered light resistance. We actively patrol the areas and are feeling the monotony of the work: collecting prisoners, checking them in, and waiting for an announcement of war's end in Western Europe. It is good to be alive, though, and it is good to know that the war here is coming to a close, with the Pacific as our next objective.

While we were sorting through prisoner records today, I witnessed something that caught me off guard; I shouldn't be surprised knowing the end is near, but it still was a bit surreal. A convoy of German trucks entered our command post, at least a dozen in a row. The trucks were full of enemy soldiers, but their approach was not aggressive, so it did not cause us to be on full alert. An officer got out of the forward most truck, and he surrendered himself and all the men in the trucks. They moved silently from their trucks and assembled into a unit.

I was struck by how the men still marched in formation until they got to the point of check-in; then they stood silently in a single line as we checked them in and recorded their names. Here were men giving in to defeat, and they were not causing any trouble. They were different from what we might have imagined when it comes to the enemy.

Not every German soldier was a Nazi; in fact, not every soldier was even German. Over the past year, we have checked in many "German soldiers" who were really prisoners of war who had been forced to fight for Germany (this flies in the face of Geneva Convention regulations, but we are not naive enough to believe all Germany POW camps would be in compliance). Over the past year, these prisoners have been very helpful in providing intel, location, and details about the enemy's plans. This has changed my attitude towards the prisoners I see because I truly cannot consider each to be my enemy.

Many of the men we put in our own POW camps were not politically driven and were not Nazi fanatics either. They were simply soldiers of their country. I understand that they may have even disagreed with Hitler's plans to eliminate all Jews. I believe that some of these men felt that disobeying orders meant certain death and believed they had no escape. I can understand those feelings.

However, aside from the POWs forced to fight for Hitler, I have difficulty, at this point in the war, justifying German military service. Perhaps an enlisted soldier in 1939 was unaware of the horrific death camps and mass murders, but now, in 1945, it is not possible to plead ignorance. In my mind, a man who chooses to continue the fight for Germany, with full knowledge of Hitler's barbarity, is not a true soldier. A soldier's job is to protect the innocent, sacrificing his own life if necessary. In continuing to fight this war, the enemy soldier is choosing his life over the oppressed citizens of his own country. That is unacceptable to me.

After seeing, first hand, the subcamp of Dachau and realizing that Auschwitz and other camps were employing the same techniques on an even larger scale, I cannot accept any involvement, even if it is a blind acceptance of the Nazi's actions. Did all of the German soldiers participate in executions? Certainly not. Did they know what was happening by this point in the war, and are therefore complicit? Absolutely.

Steadfast and Loyal,
Uncle Jim

MAY 9, 1945

Dear Rose,

Yesterday, we were given official word that Germany has surrendered. We knew it was coming. Hitler had committed suicide on April 30. He knew he could not win, and he knew what would be done to him if he were captured alive. We anticipated this.

At word of the surrender, there was a lot of celebrating among civilians. It is understakable how the people of Europe must feel after six years of war, of rations, of air raids, of oppression. The party that erupted in Paris when it was liberated was now taking place throughout Europe. Though, this time, we, the troops, were a little more guarded in our rejoicing.

The war in Europe is over, but the war in the Pacific is not. Too many of our boys are still fighting a fierce war in the Pacific, so the news of German surrender carries bittersweet emotions with it.

Additionally, it all feels a bit anticlimactic as the war has not left us undamaged. There have been so many terrible experiences during this war: the men we have lost, the enemy we have killed, hedgerow fighting, the frozen hell of the forest, miserable weather, dangerous terrain, concentration camps, hunger, fear. It all has taken a toll on us, physically and mentally.

And it isn't over yet.

We have been put on occupational duty, and we won't be going home. We will stay to disarm, restore order, and rebuild. We have to process prisoners and establish a temporary military government. There are refugees and displaced citizens to reintroduce and emergency shelters to guard. There are water supplies, electricity, and gas to restore. Then, at some point, we will be sent back to the States, but not to go home permanently. We will be given 30 days rest and then will join each other again at an Army camp on the east coast. There, we will train and wait to be deployed for the Pacific where the war still rages on.

Therefore, yesterday, we celebrated. But today, we know there is much more to endure. I will write more soon.

Steadfast and Loyal,
Uncle Jim

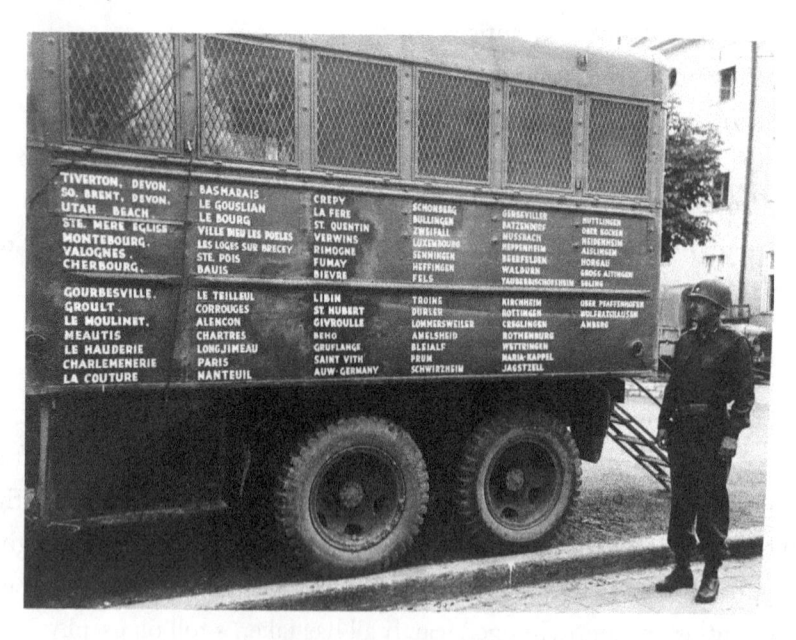

Truck listing the 4th Division's engagements during European campaign, found among Uncle Jim's mementos.

COLONEL POOL OFFICIALLY WELCOMES GENERAL RODWELL—Col. Herbert M. Pool, post commander at Camp Butner greets Brig. Gen. James Rodwell, right, assistant commander of the Fourth Infantry Division with a hearty handshake in his office Saturday morning. The bemedaled veteran of two wars arrived here late Friday evening to take charge of the advance party of the Ivy Division scheduled to arrive here within a few days. —U. S. Army Signal Corps Photo.

Gen. Rodwell Arrives At Camp Butner

Assistant Chief Takes Charge Of Ivy Advance Party

Brig. Gen. James S. Rodwell, assistant commander of the Fourth Infantry, arrived at Camp Butner late Friday evening to take charge of the advance party of the Ivy Division scheduled to arrive here about Aug. 8. He was greeted by Col. George M. O'Connor, commanding officer of the 28th Detachment Headquarters, and Headquarters, Special Troops, Second Army, after motoring in from his home in Rio Grande City, Texas.

The assistant commander was officially greeted to Camp Butner by Col. Herbert M. Pool, post commander, at 9 A. M. today. They discussed plans for the housing of the Fourth.

General Rodwell said that he expected the first cadre to arrive would be made up of 141 enlisted men and 44 officers, representatives of all the units. It is their job to greet each organization and see that they are taken to the right area. They must also provide a plan for training for the units.

General Rodwell said that expected the commanding general of the Fourth, Major General Blakely, to arrive about Aug. 13. He added that the main part of the division would start reporting in shortly thereafter.

A veteran of both World War I and II, General Rodwell came into the Army June 22 when the Ivy Division was reactivated. The bemedaled veteran now holds the Distinguished Service Cross, Silver Star with an Oak Leaf Cluster, the Bronze Star, Pre-Pearl Harbor Ribbon, European Theatre of Operations Ribbon with five battle stars and an arrowhead for participation in the invasion of France, British Distinguished Service Order, the French Legion of Honor and the French Croix de Guerre for this war. He has the Victory Medal with five battle stars for World War I and the Occupation of Germany during World War I.

With General Rodwell was his wife. They plan to reside on the post until accommodations can be found in Durham.

Newspaper clipping, August 1945, detailing training at Camp Butner where the 4th Division would train under General Blakeley in preparation for deployment to the Pacific. Found in Uncle Jim's scrapbook.

Beth Rieman is in St. Marie du Mont, France

June 25, 2019 at 10:00 pm • St. Marie du Mont, France

The Ivy House and views from my window

Town center, St. Marie du Mont, Severine, Charles, Véronique at restaurant

Monument in the center of town, Famous picture in front of same monument

I can't believe I am here! I am here, in France, to donate the cane! I made it to Normandy around 6:00pm (France time) today after many airport issues, and after landing in Paris around 1:00pm. It was quite the experience but that only added to the journey. I met some people I would not have otherwise met and had lunch at a professor's home near Paris with some very interesting people. It felt like being in a movie, some sort of great adventure. I am trying hard to take everything in, remember every single moment of this journey, and feel every emotion, but I am also really tired as I write this!

St. Marie du Mont is a town preserved, like stepping into the 1940s. There are no advertisements, no neon lights, nothing that blatantly allows you to sense commercialism or modern advances. The buildings have kept their original appearances, architecture that is very old by our standards. The town itself is exactly how I imagined it. It is untouched, quiet, and peaceful.

Driving down the roads, you are surrounded by mounds of earth and vegetation. The roads are narrow and, if a car approaches in the opposite direction, you have to pull over to make room (no wonder, during WWII, tanks had difficulty passing through). Sometimes the vegetation on the sides of the roads are the ancient hedgerows present during the Normandy Invasion. Sometimes, the tree branches, on either side of the road, lean over and form arches, so you are driving through a sort of tunnel. There are apple trees and clusters of cows and horses along the way. It is just beautiful.

Everywhere you go, you are reminded of the invasion. Marks from bullets are purposely preserved in the walls, floors, and streets. Painstaking renovation is underway for the beautiful church that stands in the center of town, but the interior still shows marks of the war, and it will be kept that way. Plaques are mounted everywhere in the town to mark various landmarks and there are signs to explain 1944's events. You see flags proudly displayed everywhere you go, and wherever a French flag is flown, there is also an American. There is a deep sense of gratitude among the people here. They have not forgotten the sacrifice so many made for their freedom.

This evening the curator of the museum, Charles, and his wife, Véronique, picked me up and took me to dinner where we joined the museum director, Severine. The monument in the center of town is in honor of family members (and men in the town) who died in WWI; a famous picture of the 101st Airborne was taken in front of it in 1944. They made sure to recreate this in the TV mini-series Band of Brothers as well. This monument was next to the restaurant so Charles showed his relatives' names inscribed on it before we went inside. His family lost many to WWI and sacrificed much in WWII as well; they are a significant part of the town's history.

Charles' father built the museum and he is very emotionally tied to it. I am amazed at the story of his family. Michel (Charles' father) was 23 years old on D-Day; after American soldiers destroyed hidden German artillery on his family's farm, Michel approached American soldiers with a white handkerchief to speak to them, but they did not see the flag and assumed he was an enemy. A soldier shot him five times, seriously wounding him. After the soldier realized his mistake, Michel was rushed to a first aid station on the beach and evacuated to England to receive care. He spent eight months in an English hospital, and survived, but, as a result of his injuries, he was unable to perform physical labor or work on his family's farm when he returned. After all this, he never held a grudge.

One of the American soldiers who had taken out the artillery on the family farm toured France decades after the war and stopped at Brecourt Manor where he met Michel and talked with him. Michel never fully knew the details of the battle or even why Americans were on the family farm that day. When it was all explained to him, he knew he had to create the museum. He struggled to convince the people of the town, who wanted to forget the war as best they could, but he didn't give up. He founded the museum to preserve the memory of D-Day and honor the actions of the brave people who liberated their town, and he made sure the location was in the exact place where the troops had landed on D-Day.

I was really moved by this story as well as the fact that Charles is continuing his father's legacy by running the museum and adding to the collections.

We had dinner in a restaurant where every dish was prepared with a crepe in some form or another; my meal had a dark crepe underneath ham and potatoes. I was able to sample the cider that is made in this region too. Everything was so fresh and well prepared. We had a lovely evening learning about each other, and we ended with conversation about Uncle Jim and Teddy Roosevelt, Jr. The entire team at the museum is beyond moved to have the cane and we cried talking about how important Teddy Roosevelt is to this town, how the people here feel that he was instrumental in liberating them from the four years of German occupation. There is a sense of awe and reverence here when people are told who the cane belonged to and how it was passed on. They are really, truly honored by receiving the cane which, of course, lets us know this is where it should be.

This whole experience is exactly as I hoped, where every single moment, every breath, every word, feels special. I can feel a presence here too, which is not really something I have ever felt before; it is like loved ones are with me and are watching the circle close. It is incredible.

I need to sleep to have a clearer mind, so I will try to explain more when I have had more than two hours of sleep. For now, I am heading to bed.

Charles' father who was mistaken for a German and shot on D-Day. He forgave the American responsible and established the museum in 1962 to honor the sacrifices of those who fought for France's freedom. Utah Beach Museum

Beth Rieman is in Colleville-sur-Mer, France
June 26, 2019 at 10:00 am • Colleville-sur-Mer, France

Sand Ceremony

Teddy Roosevelt, Jr's grave with cane and flowers

It is a cold, rainy morning. There is a mist in the air, which I think you can see in the pictures. It gives everything a somewhat pensive, wistful look that feels very appropriate for what we are doing. Charles, and a friend from the museum, Flavie (who I absolutely adore), picked me up and took me to the American cemetery. We brought flowers from Charles' home, Brecourt Manor.

When we got to the cemetery, we discovered that Teddy Roosevelt's grave was sectioned off in order for the grass to recover from the 75th Anniversary celebration a few weeks prior. Visitors were not allowed in the area near his grave. Charles was very gracious and sought the help of the cemetery's curator and we were met by two men who provided a covered golf cart to take us to Roosevelt's grave, making an exception for us. The men were so gracious and kind, and they had an excited energy, feeling fortunate to be working today so that they could be part of the experience. (They kept asking to hold the cane and were speechless; the looks on their faces filled my heart.)

A little backstory so you understand what is happening in the pictures and video…Teddy Roosevelt's brother, Quentin, was killed in action in France during WWI. His body was buried in Chamery, France, about 300 miles from here. When the American Cemetery was built in France, and Teddy Roosevelt was buried, the Roosevelt family had Quentin's remains moved to be buried next to Teddy. Their crosses are at the front of the rows in their section and just beyond their graves, you can see the threshold of land where it meets Omaha beach. It is very poetic to see their crosses next to each other, two Presidential sons who paid the ultimate sacrifice.

The cemetery interpretive guide honored us with a sand ceremony for Quentin which you can watch here (https://www.youtube.com/watch?v=Vqa5gRmcgW4&feature=youtu.be). Sand from Omaha beach is rubbed onto the cross where the words have been carved into the stone. (They cannot do this for Teddy Roosevelt because his cross inscription has gold inlaid since he is a Medal of Honor recipient.) The excess sand is then brushed off, once inside the inscription, and the remaining sand allows the name and details to stand out against the white cross. Next, French and American flags are placed in the ground, the tradition being that the American flag be placed closest to the ocean, and the French flag placed closest to the land (symbolic for 1944's positions).

After the sand ceremony, flags were also placed on Teddy Roosevelt's grave and we all stood silently for a moment, taking it all in: the significance of the ceremony, the image of two crosses bearing the names of brothers who lay side-by-side in eternal rest, the emotions of all that has come to pass. We placed Charles' flowers on Teddy's grave and that felt even more emotional. Flowers from the location of the battle that took place on Charles' family's farm were now with the leader of the infantry who stormed the beach before linking up with the soldiers who fought at Brecourt Manor. Here they were, meeting again. Just as significant are the flowers' connection with Charles' father, whose forgiveness and gesture of gratitude is incredibly inspirational.

Finally, the last step...With the flags and flowers in place, we put the cane against Teddy Roosevelt's cross and quietly left it there to rest for a while. No one was near us while we stood in respect since we were the only people allowed in the area which had been roped off that day.

It is indescribable, the way that felt. What a journey the cane has been on, the things it has seen, the lives it has touched...And now, the cane has come full circle to be reunited with its owner. As we stood there, lost in thought and emotion, it was quiet, peaceful, and deeply personal. Everyone cried.

I was given the flags that were placed on both graves to take with me, and I will treasure them as a memory of this day. Charles said this was an experience that will stay in his heart forever...as it will mine.

A quote from one of my mom's favorite movies seems very appropriate for this moment: "There will never be another day like today."

▇▇▇▇▇▇▇▇▇▇▇▇▇▇▇▇▇▇   Mon, Jul 1, 2019, 5:46 AM
to me

Good Morning Ms. Rieman,

I hope you don't mind but I submitted an article to our in-house staff magazine on the subject of your visit to the cemetery last week. I have attached a copy for your retention and I hope that it meets with your approval.

It was such an occasion with historical magnitude that you will appreciate why we were bowled over by your visit. Thank you for your consideration in this matter. We also met at the flag ceremony that same evening, Mr. Bill McIntyre a veteran who you met on Utah Beach that same morning. He spoke volumes of your meeting and like us was privileged to hold the cane.

Should you require any other service from the ABMC staff here at Normandy, then please do not hesitate to ask.

Kind Regards,

Anthony ▇▇▇▇ (Interpretive Guide).

Email received, from American Cemetery in Normandy (with attached article)

ABMC STAFF MAGAZINE
A VISIT TO THE ROOSEVELT BROTHERS

Ms. Rieman, standing by T. Roosevelt Jr's grave

Certain days in our lives are indeed special and unique and Wednesday, 26th June, 2019 will rank amongst their numbers. A day of managed routine in many ways in the Normandy American Cemetery, with talks, tours and visitor feedback by the Guide team. Then at about 10:45 AM on a misty, windy and generally melancholic morning (when we had been promised a "canicule"!) all changed by one simple radio statement to the Guides sat at the Welcome Desk by Alain Dupain, one of our gardening supervisors. "Can someone help out a lady in the area of the Memorial? She would like to visit the Roosevelts' graves and she has in her possession Theodore Roosevelt Junior's cane!" Anthony Lewis, Interpretive Guide, shot out of his chair and had collected sand, sponge and two sets of the American and French flags within seconds.

A message was relayed to Alain stating that the guides (Anthony and Alan Roptin, a seasonal guide), were on their way. They scorched their way by golf cart to the Memorial (paying due care to our visitors) to be informed that the party concerned were making their way to the flag poles. They divided resources with Alan going ahead on foot to meet the party and Anthony re-siting the golf cart position for easy pick-up. They met a party of an American lady, a French lady, and a French gentleman. After introductions were exchanged, they were on their way to Plot D's last row (Row 28) and indeed the last two graves (Graves 45 & 46). The plot was amongst five others off limits to the general public to give it an opportunity to recover after 6th June ceremony.

Ms. Rieman, who was in possession of the cane, explained that her great uncle was Brigadier General James S. Rodwell and in the 4th U.S Infantry Division with Teddy Roosevelt. They were great personal friends. On the day of Theodore Roosevelt Junior's death from his third heart attack 12th July 1944, General Rodwell was given the cane. He carried it in honor of his friend through the rest of the European campaign. It was with him at Saint-Lô, as the 4th Division entered Paris when it was liberated, in the Battle of the Bulge and the Hurtgen Forest. It had remained in her family ever since and had been authenticated in the United States. It was also the subject of press articles. As James Rodwell was her great grandfather's brother and had no children, his important

Anthony and Alan standing by T. Roosevelt's grave

memorabilia were passed to her grandmother and then to her mother.

A number of photographs were taken to memorialize the occasion at the gravesites of both brothers – Quentin and Theodore Roosevelt Junior after the graves had been sanded and flagged in the traditional cemetery manner. Both guides asked permission to hold this historic cane and were allowed to be photographed with it. Such opportunities are exceptionally rare and they were honored to handle this unique historical artifact. It was after such a heartening experience that the cane was returned to its owner, who was in turn about to hand it over to the Utah Beach museum owner.

Ms. Rieman thanked the guides by mail for her incredible experience on the day. "It is one that is a highlight of my life, something that will forever live in my heart". And so say all of us!

Beth Rieman is in St.Marie du Mont, France

June 26, 2019 at 12:00 pm • St. Marie du Mont, France

Utah Beach

Together with Charles, Flavie, and Benoit (head of historical research and collections for the museum), we took the cane to the site of the D-Day beach invasion. As soon as we stepped foot on the sand, we were met by a 99-year old veteran from Texas, Bill McIntyre, who had been here that fateful day in 1944. He shared stories of his service and I explained the significance of the cane, which of course received a reaction of astonishment. He held the cane and got choked up. He told stories he had heard of Teddy Roosevelt (though not part of the same division as he), and he spontaneously saluted when holding the cane. I can't help but think that I was SUPPOSED to meet this man today as yet another unexpected moment that added to an already moving experience. I cried once again and hugged Mr. McIntyre as he and his family left the beach.

Then, I was able to walk the cane to the precise location where Teddy Roosevelt, Jr, on D-Day, landed with the first wave of troops. I stood with my back to the ocean, looking over the sand and up the seawall, imagining what it would have looked like, what it would have felt like, to be here on D-Day (https://m.youtube.com/watch?v=_T65K_pGMZgkn). I know there is no way for me to truly feel what a soldier would have felt that day, the sights he would have seen, the courage it would have taken, but I was still filled with emotion as I stood reverently. I said a prayer for Teddy Roosevelt, Jr, for Uncle Jim, for the veteran I had just met, and for all the men and women who were there that day.

Then, I walked with the cane, letting its base sink into the sand, a distinct awareness that I was doing this almost exactly 75 years after Teddy Roosevelt, Jr would have been plodding along the same shore, cane in his hand, directing the troops. I was holding the handle of his cane where he once held it (and where Uncle Jim once held it too), and I was following the path he once took.

Each step and each placement of the cane was intensely meaningful to me. To know that the cane was touching the same sand, tracing the same steps, and finally coming to rest in the same place, was very emotional, and once again, my eyes filled with tears.

Beth Rieman is in St. Marie du Mont, France

June 26, 2019 at 1:00 pm • St. Marie du Mont, France

Brecourt Manor

We returned to Charles' house, Brecourt Manor, from where he picked the flowers to take to the cemetery, so that he could share his family's story. If you have never heard of Brecourt Manor, to put it lightly, what happened here was critical in securing the success of the Utah Beach invasion. Paratroopers of the 101st Airborne Division were dropped behind enemy lines, hours before the first wave of infantry landed on the beach; the objective for the paratroopers was to secure the marsh areas beyond the beach and block key routes to the beach that could be used by German reinforcements. After completing their objective, the 101st Airborne planned to meet the 4th Infantry Division (Teddy Roosevelt's and Uncle Jim's division) inland after the 4th Infantry Division had cleared the beach and passed the seawall (the two groups of soldiers were invading in opposite directions, and then moving forward to meet in the middle).

Like everything else on D-Day, things didn't go quite as planned. The paratroopers landed away from their target, separated from each other, and managed to gather only 100 out of the men assigned. Of that 100, the majority of the soldiers were sent to secure the routes to the beach while Easy Company's 14 remaining men were sent to eliminate enemy artillery hidden in the vegetation at Brecourt Manor (the artillery the Germans had hidden was aimed to reach Utah Beach, designed to kill the men who would be landing there). Easy Company's commander died when his plane was hit by Germans, so they were led by their Lieutenant who designed a very successful plan to eliminate the hidden weapons and save countless lives in doing so. Astonishingly, though dropped off course…after being lost…after being separated…with one-tenth of the men needed to accomplish this objective…and after intense fighting, they neutralized the German artillery at Brecourt Manor. Had they not, the men landing on Utah Beach would have suffered many more casualties while accomplishing their mission.

Because Brecourt Manor was made even more famous by the HBO series, Band of Brothers (specifically episode 2), tourists often drive to the manor to look at it from the outside and to see the field where everything happened. The field is gated, locked, and surrounded by electric fencing to keep people from trespassing. Charles and his family live at Brecourt Manor (a home that has been in his family for many generations) and own the adjoining field where the German artillery was hidden, the field where the 101st Airborne Division fought to destroy the artillery.

When we drove to Brecourt Manor, I did not realize where I was being taken. I thought I was going to drive past an area where a scene was filmed. Lost in translation? Clueless? Not sure what the case was, but it didn't sink in that I was getting special treatment until later. Once we arrived, Charles turned off the electric fence, unlocked the gate, and took me onto the field. He explained, point by point, the details of what happened in 1944 while drawing my attention to various locations around the field. He showed me where the artillery would have been hidden, where the German trenches would have been dug, and where the paratroopers would have fought.

You guys, I was standing on the field where it all happened, just Charles, Flavie, me...and the cows!!! No one gets to do this!!!! Tourists can look but are kept from coming onto the field by the electric fence. BUT...I got to be right there, learning more about D-Day...learning about how incredibly brave Easy Company's men were and how amazing it was that they succeeded in helping the infantry on the beaches...learning about producers'/actors' visits while making Band of Brothers...even learning about the details that were portrayed inaccurately in the series (Especially the cows. They used the wrong type of cows. This does not please Charles lol). I could imagine every moment, every detail, and like everything else today, I was filled with a lot of emotion. It was a very powerful moment.

After standing where history happened, that alone enough to leave my jaw dropped and my adrenaline pumping, Charles took me on a tour of the manor itself——as in, entering the gate, past what anyone is allowed to see!!!! The manor has been Charles' family's home for many generations, part of it built before the French Revolution. During the war, Germans occupied the home and had the family remain on the property so that they could supply milk from their farm. German soldiers lined the family's 36 horses in the road and shot them all so that they could not be used as transportation by the Allied forces (It is difficult to imagine four years of enemy occupation and the misery that accompanied). Just before D-Day, the family grew concerned over the behavior of the Germans, so they went into hiding in an outbuilding on the property. They remained hidden until after the fighting and came out, in shock, to see bodies, dead animals, and damage. It was here that Charles' father was mistaken for a German and shot five times by an American soldier. So much happened here—the occupation, the battle, the mistake, and the ultimate forgiveness.

Inside the home, Charles pointed out several bullet marks, a blood stain still visible on the floor, a gash in a windowsill. Juxtaposed against this evidence of the German occupation, there were also gorgeous details within the home: beautiful hand-painted floor tiles, old stone walls that would have been constructed over 200 years ago, ornate ironwork that curved up the stairs, murals Charles' grandfather painted on wall panels, an intricately carved fireplace that took up an entire wall of the dining area…it was all very impressive. (Charles asked me not to share pictures of the interior, sorry). I feel very special to have been given an inside glimpse of his family's history and I was left in awe.

Lastly, Charles took me into his own home on the manor (equally beautiful) and had me sign a poster he has had others sign over the years: Dick Winters, presidents, favorite veterans, people he has met along the way who share a connection with the town of St. Marie Du Mont and Utah Beach. It was such an honor to write my name among the others and to read all the signatures, realizing how fortunate I am to be considered a connection among so many greats.

The time spent at Brecourt Manor was yet another of the many things I am experiencing that makes this trip unbelievable. I did not expect to experience so much, to be treated so generously, or to even see things that were not related directly to the cane. I really thought I would be finding my own way to the places I knew the cane had been and venturing out on my own for anything else I might have time to see. That has not been the case. Every moment of my trip has been filled with history and amazement (and a lot of tears) and I didn't have to figure any of it out on my own. They are all such wonderful people…

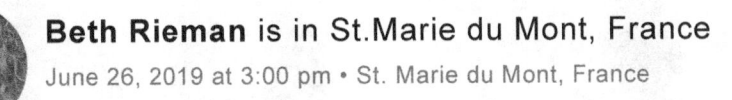

Beth Rieman is in St.Marie du Mont, France
June 26, 2019 at 3:00 pm • St. Marie du Mont, France

The Chapelle de la Madeleine, WWII photograph

The Chapelle de la Madeleine, today

Yet another perk of spending time with Charles is the fact that as deputy mayor/museum curator, he has keys to buildings not always open to the public. One of the places closed for the day was the Chapelle de la Madeleine.

This quaint church was originally built in the year 900 by a Viking King and rebuilt in the 16th century using the ruins of the original. In 1944, the chapel was an old, unused sanctuary, occupied by the Germans. The night before the D-Day invasion, two people in the town risked their lives and sabotaged the German phone lines at the chapel in order to help the Allied soldiers who would be arriving; there is a commemorative plaque on the altar in their honor (one of the men was shot 10 days after the phone lines were cut). Fortunately, the Allies captured the chapel from the Germans, but the church was badly damaged in the invasion, as you can see in the black and white photograph. Also, in the field located near the chapel, was one of the first temporary American cemeteries, with 250 graves. As you can imagine, with a church this old and with so much relevance, the community wanted to preserve its history. Funding for renovations after the war was difficult to obtain, though, because larger churches were given priority.

Enter Jean Schwob d'Hericourt. He landed on Utah Beach, after D-Day, with the French Free Forces, and the damaged Chapelle de la Madeleine was the first building he saw. On that day he vowed, if he survived the war, to help restore the church. And he did. He had a stained-glass window made in honor of the French Free Forces (not seen in pictures) and even made sure that the new bell was created by melting bronze from the former bell that dated back to 1676, taken from the destroyed belfry. Now the chapel is fully restored, Jean Schwob d'Hericourt having kept the promise he made in 1944.

I was present in this chapel without any tourists or strangers around, able to take it all in. I was standing, once again, where history happened. I could imagine the people in this town, oppressed by occupation, longing to be free, working to sabotage the phone lines. I could feel Jean Schwob d'Hericourt's triumph when he saw the chapel and knew that the people of France would soon experience liberation. The sacrifices that so many made to help people they had never known is remarkable to consider. Standing in this chapel, my mind was filled with all these things.

I am not sure I can help you all experience this vicariously, because I can't adequately put any of this into words. I have been having difficulty, all day today, describing the feelings I am having as I stand in these places and imagine the past, letting the historical significance soak into my soul. I have been feeling incredibly powerful emotions from the moment I stepped foot in Normandy.

Beth Rieman is in St.Marie du Mont, France
June 26, 2019 at 4:00 pm • St. Marie du Mont, France

Meautis

Last on the list of "musts" for the cane was the town of Meautis,

15 minutes southeast of St. Marie du Mont. The 4th Infantry Division headquarters were here briefly, as the Allied forces pushed into other areas of France after D-Day.

Some of the soldiers of the 4th Infantry Division turned a captured German truck into Teddy Roosevelt's "HQ on wheels" and parked it in a field in Meautis, near the command post. They painted the truck's interior white, hung an electric bulb, and gave Teddy a bed, desk, and space for his footlocker. Teddy slept in this truck and enjoyed it in times he was able to be alone. On July 12, 1944, Teddy's son, Quentin (named after Teddy's brother, Quentin, whose cross was used for the sand ceremony) visited him here in the evening for a few hours. Teddy confessed to Quentin that, on D-Day and since, he had been having small heart attacks, and was very tired and weak. He had seen the army doctor a few days prior and was told that his "issues were from putting an inhuman strain on a machine that was not exactly new." Quentin urged his father to rest and take some time to feel better, but wrote to his mother that he knew his words had no effect. When Quentin left a few hours later, Teddy Roosevelt went to sleep in his HQ on wheels and died of a heart attack around midnight.

Charles, Flavie, and Benoit drove me to Meautis and helped locate the area where the truck would have been parked that day. Benoit knew that the command post was at the parsonage of the church and that Teddy Roosevelt died in the field adjacent the command post (field seen in the picture). We spent some time trying to figure out which of the buildings would have been the command post because we were comparing a small section of a picture of Teddy Roosevelt from that day and could not match it. We spoke with an older woman in the town and she assured Benoit that he had the correct area. Several buildings have since been remodeled and the parsonage was one of those. So, we leaned the cane against the door of the remodeled structure (now apartments), knowing that it was the same place the picture of Teddy Roosevelt was taken on the day of his death. (We realize now that our cane does not appear to be the same cane as in the picture we were matching; however, the cane would have been in France on that day, perhaps in Teddy's HQ on wheels, near him on the night he died). As we stood back and looked at the doorway, we knew the cane was resting in one of the last places its original owner had been...and we were coming to the end of the trail, having taken the cane to all the important places.

Beth Rieman is in St. Marie du Mont, France.

June 26, 2019 at 6:00 pm • St. Marie du Mont, France

Museum Ceremony

We have come to the reason for my visit to France: donating the cane. The museum held a ceremony for the donation and press was there to interview and to commemorate the occasion. We stood in front of the Teddy Roosevelt display for the ceremony, where the cane will be displayed (circled area in picture is where the cane will be added). I was given a French and American flag that was flown over Utah Beach until the morning of June 6, 2019 (the 75th anniversary). I was given a medal commemorating D-Day and a museum book that Charles signed with a personal message. And, most importantly, I was given new friends who, for the past few days, shared meals and opened their homes to me, drove me around the entire Normandy area, and shared many stories of their own families' experiences during WWII. At the close of the ceremony, the cane passed hands from me to the museum, and it finally made its way back home.

It was strange to let the cane go, as I had been carrying it with me nonstop for three days, and it even felt a little sad, but it also felt exactly as it should be. After taking the cane to the American cemetery, to the landing site on Utah Beach, to the field in which Teddy Roosevelt died in his "HQ on wheels," and after meeting so many people who share a sense of awe when it comes to the cane, I know that many more people will know its story now.

Teddy Roosevelt, Jr. is the most honored hero in this area of France. In America, I often have to explain who he was, and even then, I am sometimes met with indifference. Here, it is a very different situation. As I carried the cane from place to place and met so many interesting people, the cane was like a celebrity. People wanted to touch it, just for a moment. People were in awe of simply being near it. People held it and cried. The townspeople here have a history deeply rooted in the sacrifices so many brave men and women made, so much so that our flag still flies next to theirs, 75 years later. There is a deep gratitude for Teddy Roosevelt, Jr. who is the hero who moved forward with the D-Day invasion, even though troops landed off course, and helped to free the people of this town. Without him, their lives would be very different.

As I shared the cane and helped continue its journey, inevitably, I would be asked how it had come to be in my possession. Incredibly, this always brought Uncle Jim's story to the surface, so another legacy was shared. In honoring his dear friend, by carrying his cane throughout the European campaign, Uncle Jim became part of the cane's story too. I felt so proud and honored to be of his blood and to be able to share his legacy. During the ceremony at the museum, Charles told me that, in addition to displaying the cane prominently, they will be telling Uncle Jim's story. They will be displaying photographs of him, recognizing his service, and allowing others to know his part of the cane's journey. They will be doing this because his life, to all of them, and of course to me, is as meaningful as the cane's connection to Teddy Roosevelt, Jr. I did not expect this, and I am so pleased that Brigadier General James S. Rodwell will have a place in history, right next to Brigadier General Teddy Roosevelt, Jr., with their story of friendship on display for others to know.

When Charles shared this plan, I realized that the cane's story did not stop when the war ended in 1945, and the cane's story was not solely connected to Teddy Roosevelt, Jr's legacy. The story's chapters continued to be written by my Uncle Jim...and then by my Grandma Rose...and even by my family as we unpacked her boxes. Furthermore, over the past few days, the chapters continued to be written by Charles, Severine, Flavie, Benoit, and me as we took the cane on its last physical journey. How awesome that, in this way, we are all now part of the cane's story. I can't think of a better ending to this life changing journey.

Beth Rieman is in Delaware, Ohio
June 30, 2019 at 12:00 pm • Delaware, OH

Cane comparison

I am home now and I can't stop thinking about my whirlwind trip to France. I am not sure anything will ever come close to that experience. I went online to download all my pictures and I found this picture of

Teddy Roosevelt, Jr. in 1927, meeting with disabled men, using the cane. To think of the things that cane has seen, the places it has been, and the lives it has touched, brings tears that roll down my cheeks. It has finally come to rest with its beloved owner … and with the men he led from the front, the men who, like Teddy and Uncle Jim, gave everything to fight for others' freedoms.

JIM

AUGUST 14, 1945

Dear Rose,

When we heard the news, a spontaneous cheer erupted. The Allies are victorious and the enemies have surrendered. The preparations under way for the invasion of Japan can be cancelled. Hats were tossed into the air, men embraced in bear hugs, and there was a happy commotion.

The cheers were followed with a sense of relief.

And then, the smiles started to fade.

Everyone began to quiet their voices. There was a shuffling of feet, eyes looking at the ground, no one really knowing what to say. I looked around at the men of the 4th Infantry Division and many of them seemed to be sort of disoriented, sort of lost.

I knew what was happening. Of course, we were happy the war was over, but the happiness came at a cost. And the cost was playing like a movie reel in our minds. The men we had lost. The destruction. The civilians affected and the horrific devastation. We couldn't talk about it then; I'm not sure we ever will. I think we all realize that, in order to survive the horrors of war, we need to move forward and avoid any time spent looking back.

What does "forward" look like, though, for these men? What does a return to normalcy mean for men who are returning from war? They have spent every waking and sleeping moment together. They have shared their stories, their worries, and their tears. Together, they have reached into the pits of their souls and dug out every ounce of bravery. They are different men than the men they were before the war. And now, they return to their homes, to people who will never—and can never—understand what they have experienced. They must return without the only people who do understand, without the men who have become their family over the course of this war. Their Army brothers are scattering to separate corners of the country, and they feel a different kind of loss now.

I share some of the same feelings, but I have made a career of this, and I will not be going home alone. I will have many Army brothers in my daily life, men with whom I share these experiences. I will get to see Tubby and work with him still. This brings me comfort and I know I am one of the lucky ones.

What I do think about now is the men we left in Europe who will never get to cope with mixed feelings about returning to their homes. So many fallen soldiers. The anguish of it all. Yet without the war, our brotherhood would not have developed. We were all brought together by combat, and, right or wrong, good or bad, we came out of it as brothers.

Which makes me think of Ted.

I suppose, in this way, I am feeling what the other men feel. In France, I grieved the loss of my friend, but the magnitude of the war and the velocity of its pace allowed me to compartmentalize my thoughts and push my mourning to the side for the job I had to do. I know that I have not fully digested it. Suddenly, I realize that, like my mother, my father, and Robert, gone too soon, Ted is too. I will have none of them in my daily life when I return home.

For all of us today, celebration over the war's end faded to this strange kind of melancholy.

Another casualty of war.

As I begin to process these feelings, my mind plays a memory of Ted. He passes by, wearing his garrison cap, and grinning that grin. He stops. He turns. And, raising his cane in his right hand, he salutes with it.

Steadfast and Loyal,
Uncle Jim

THEODORE ROOSEVELT JR
BRIGADIER GENERAL U S ARMY
NEW YORK JULY 12 1944

AUTHOR'S NOTE

Uncle Jim passed away in 1962, during a period when many were still reluctant to talk about their war experiences. Therefore, he is not among the men whose stories have been collected, compiled, and shared in various books, documentaries, and movies. His story, the cane's story, and the story of friendship could have been lost forever. I am glad that was not the case. I believe the details had been in boxes for far too long and were begging to be discovered, the stories longing to be told. I believe Uncle Jim had a hand in everything that came to pass since opening the first box and I am honored to have been chosen to share his legacy.

By documenting, on social media, the details as they were emerging, presenting the story to various groups, sharing with reporters, and finally donating the cane, my hope was that more people would learn about two great men, and appreciate their generation's contribution to our collective history. By writing this book, my hope is that the story's impact will reach even farther.

The social meda posts in this book were pulled directly from my personal page. The artifacts sprinkled throughout are pictures of some of the items we found as we opened boxes and paged through scrapbooks and binders. Uncle Jim and Teddy Roosevelt's entries occasionally contain words and phrases from interviews, personal letters, articles, and Army reports, but most of their words are my invention (though I did my best to match the entries to their writing styles). The historical facts embedded throughout their entries are accurate, based on my research and the documents Uncle Jim left for us. However, it should be said that, due to censorship rules for military mail, much of what is mentioned in Uncle Jim's letters, though historically accurate, would not have been written and sent in 1944 and 1945. He would certainly have followed all guidelines and would not have disclosed any sensitive information.

Overall, I believe I have painted an authentic picture of the time period, relationships, and specific battles that took place, but one will never be able to convey, with absolute certainty, the specific conversations and undocumented moments Uncle Jim and Teddy Roosevelt shared. The entries in which they interact with each other and/or speak of their friendship came from my imagination, what I believe could have happened, but I do not know them to be factual. I believe they would have shared their stories of loss and felt connected by similar experiences and I also believe they would have had a lot of fun laughing together and joking around when they had the time to do so. To the same extent, I do not know the particulars of the moment Teddy Roosevelt gave the cane to Uncle Jim because I have not found anything that documents the occasion. Through Ernie Pyle's article, the pictures of Uncle Jim with the cane, comparative analysis, etc., we have certain provenance and documentation that the cane was passed between them while they were in France in 1944. However, we do not know the conversation that took place. I have a romanticized version in my mind of an intimate conversation where Teddy Roosevelt, knowing he was nearing the end of his life, expressed his feelings and asked that Uncle Jim keep one of his canes as a reminder of their friendship, of the brotherhood shared in the Army. That is what my heart wants it to be like. Perhaps, though, the moment was much simpler, just an understanding that the cane should be his. We may never know, but I hope that with this story, I have come close to portraying their friendship in a true light.

When I was recently home again, I looked through an old album of my grandmother's. I had looked through the album before, but it is different now, after all we have learned, and after my trip to France. Several pages of the album contain pictures of Uncle Jim—with Grandma Rose, with my great-grandmother, with his wife. My grandmother has carefully labeled the pictures in short phrases that now convey new understandings. I see, through her labels, how she felt about Uncle Jim and how he was, indeed, a link to the father she never had a chance to know. I see how she is proud to be Uncle Jim's niece and proud to be a Rodwell. And, I am able to see how good-natured Uncle Jim was, how genuinely kind.

These pictures give visuals to the man who came into my family's lives, more than fifty years past his death. The last time I saw these particular pictures, I only knew that Uncle Jim was my great-grandfather's brother (my grandmother's uncle), but now he is so much more to me. In the core of my being, I know him, love him, and feel close to him, though we never met. I feel the same about Teddy Roosevelt.

I am not convinced that these connections and feelings are coincidental. While I certainly took steps to research, discover, and travel, I don't believe much of what has come to pass was completely within my control. I know that loved ones had a hand in this, and I felt their presence many times throughout the process. I hope that Uncle Jim is looking down, delighted to see that Rose's granddaughter has shared his legacy. I hope that Teddy and he are both smiling down, proud that their friendship will be immortalized with the cane's display. And I hope that my grandmother is overjoyed to know that Robert Rodwell and James Rodwell are finally so much more than just names on a family tree.

From start to finish, this has been an extraordinary journey, one I could never have imagined when I opened that first box and started to unpack yesterday.

Uncle Jim and Teddy

ADDITIONAL FACTS

Teddy Roosevelt, Jr

TEDDY ROOSEVELT, JR

Teddy Roosevelt, Jr. was the eldest son of President Theodore Roosevelt and wife, Edith. He graduated from Harvard in 1909. In 1910, he married his wife, Eleanor Butler Alexander (whom he called "Bunny") and they had four children together. He rose to the rank of Lt. Colonel in WWI, commanding the 26th Regiment of the 1st Infantry Division. He was wounded twice and gassed, his last injury sending him home to recover. Before he could return to the front, the war ended, and Teddy received several medals for his service, including the Distinguished Service Cross. He walked with the aid of a cane from that point on.

Following the First World War, Teddy entered politics. He was the Assistant Secretary of the Navy under President Harding, in 1921. In 1924, he ran for Governor of New York, but lost. He was named Governor General of the Philippines by President Hoover several years later. An avid hunter and collector, Teddy traveled to Central Asia and India to collect specimens for the Field Museum of Natural History. He and his brother were the first to discover the giant panda in the wild, enabling scientists to learn more about this animal as well as locating areas of habitat in order to gather pandas for zoos.

When Americans were attacked in Pearl Harbor, Teddy held a commission with the British Army which he immediately resigned in order to enter service in the American Army. Once again, he was with the 1st Infantry Division when he entered WWII and he was Deputy Commander of the 1st Infantry Division in Tunisia and Sicily. His son, Quentin, was also enlisted in the 1st Infantry Division and the father-son pair earned commendations for their gallantry in action in the Mediterranean; Quentin earned the Silver Star and Teddy the oak leaf cluster to his Silver Star, among other medals.

Teddy Roosevelt, Jr. and the 1st Infantry Division Commander, General Terry Allen, often clashed with superiors and did not have particularly good relationships with General Patton or General Bradley. When given the chance to replace Roosevelt and Allen, Patton and Bradley grabbed the opportunity. Teddy was removed from the 1st Infantry Division and this was a very emotional experience for him. The men of the 1st Infantry Division loved Teddy and he loved them. They were a close unit. Teddy was unable to say goodbye without tears and had to send a letter to the division to convey his feelings. Upon his removal, he put in many requests to lead assault units in Europe and even had his wife visit General Marshall to ask for his intervention. He was eventually transferred to the 4th Infantry Division and was sent to England to join their preparations for the D-Day invasion. Teddy was elated to be joining them and quickly felt at home in his new division.

On D-Day, and after several requests for permission, Teddy joined the first wave of infantry to land on Utah Beach. Armed with nothing but a 45-caliber pistol, a book of poems, and his cane, Teddy led his troops from the front and was integral in the success of the invasion. The troops landed off course and Teddy was able to regroup and continue the invasion from an alternate location. He was also able to meet with incoming waves of troops and leaders to advise of the changes and keep the causeway organized, using his cane to wave down men and give directions. For his leadership on D-Day, he was posthumously awarded the Medal of Honor.

Teddy continued to lead troops after D-Day, through hedgerow battles, and on foot to aid in the capture of Cherbourg. However, his time in WWII was cut short. On July 12, 1944, after visiting with his son, Quentin for a few hours, he retired to his HQ on wheels and died shortly before midnight. Unknown to him, a recommendation promoting him to Major General and giving him his first command of a division were on General Eisenhower's desk to be signed the next day. Teddy was buried on July 14, 1944 in the temporary cemetery in Normandy. His body was later moved to the American Cemetery in Normandy and his brother, Quentin, having died in action during WWI, was exhumed and moved from Chamery, France to the American Cemetery in Normandy, in order to be buried next to Teddy.

RAYMOND O. BARTON

Blakeley, Barton, Rodwell

Major General Raymond O. Barton (center, with Blakeley on his left and Rodwell on his right) was a career officer of the Army, beginning in WWI, when he was part of the postwar occupation in Europe, 1st Battalion Commander of the 8th Infantry Regiment, 4th Infantry Division. He was Chief of Staff of the 4th Infantry Division from 1940-1941 and Chief of Staff of the IV Army Corps the following year. On July 3, 1942, he was promoted to Commanding General of the 4th Infantry Division, at the age of fifty-three. In the Hürtgen forest, he gave his belt to be used as a tourniquet, and then awarded a Silver Star to the medic involved. Shortly after, he left his command at the end of December 1944 for health reasons. He retired from the Army in 1946, one of very few in history to command their division for the entire duration of their combat service.

ERNEST HEMINGWAY AND J.D. SALINGER

Hemingway

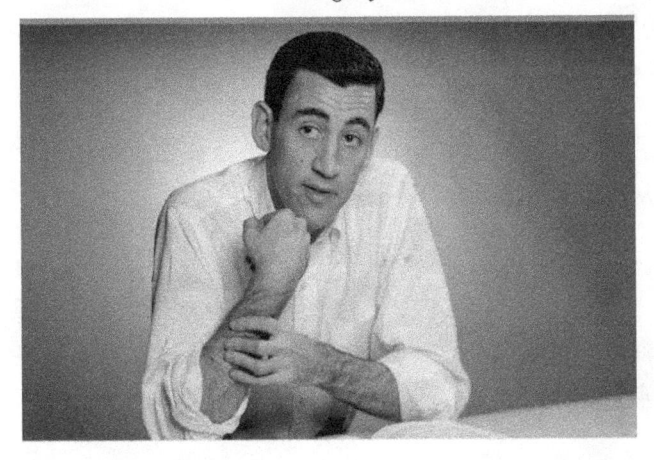

Salinger

Ernest Hemingway was encouraged by his wife to join her in Europe to write stories of the war. He was embedded with the 4th Infantry Division beginning on June 28, 1944. He and his driver, "Red," rode around France in a commandeered German motorcycle with side-car. There are many stories about Hemingway's involvement in the war, rounding up Germans in towns, and using weapons to do so (but denying it due to the laws governing war correspondents).

During the celebration of the liberation of Paris, he was met by another author, J.D. Salinger, who was enlisted in the 4th Infantry Division, with the 12th Infantry Regiment, in the Counter Intelligence Corps. Salinger admired Hemingway's work and Hemingway thought Salinger had a lot of talent. Up to this point, J.D. Salinger had published many short stories for *Collier's* and *The Saturday Evening Post*, but he was yet to publish his novel, *The Catcher in the Rye*. He was working on the character, Holden Caulfield, throughout WWII and shared many of the details with Ernest Hemingway. They once met in Hemingway's cabin in the middle of the Hürtgen Forest and drank champagne from canteen cups as they discussed Salinger's ideas. J.D. Salinger was carrying rough drafts of at least six chapters of *The Catcher in the Rye* throughout the war.

He was forever haunted by his experiences during the war, especially what he saw in concentration camps, and had a mental breakdown when the war ended; he was treated in a Nuremberg hospital for "battle fatigue," which we now call PTSD.

SLAPTON SANDS

Slapton Sands

The area in England from which citizens were evacuated, called Slapton Sands, was used for amphibious training because its terrain closely resembled that of the beaches in Normandy. On April 28, 1944, one of the rehearsals there quickly became catastrophic. A convoy of eight LSTs (Landing Ship Tanks) containing vehicles and combat engineers was attacked by German E-boats who had been patrolling the area and noticed their movement.

The LSTs were on different frequencies from the British Navy so the British were unable to alert the Americans and did not send reinforcements in time to protect the convoy. Various LSTs were torpedoed, set on fire, etc. and the casualties were numerous. Many men, floating in the water, died of hypothermia while they waited to be rescued. Others drowned because they had not been properly trained to put their lifebelts around their packs. The only area not covered by their packs was their waist, and in wearing the belts there, the weight of their packs flipped them upside down, dragging their heads underwater and drowning them.

As a result, the government ordered a complete black out of information (not revealed for another forty-four years). Everyone involved was sworn to secrecy and no information could be discussed in letters home or otherwise. Additionally, lifebelt trainings were conducted, radio frequencies were standardized, and adjustments were made to ensure the use of small boats to collect floating survivors on D-Day.

In all, at least 800 casualties were a result of the botched training exercise, ranging from men at the enlisted level through officers. Ironically, there were more casualties at Slapton Sands than there were at Utah Beach on D-Day.

UTAH BEACH MUSEUM

Utah Beach Museum

The cane is showcased in St. Marie du Mont, at The Utah Beach Museum (Musee du Debarquement), which was built on the site of the D-Day landings, in the area in which Teddy Roosevelt, Jr. and the first wave of infantry troops disembarked to spearhead the invasion. The museum's exhibits recount the D-Day invasion from its preparation to its success and contain many significant artifacts, including objects, oral histories on film, and vehicles. There is an original B26 Bomber displayed in a glass domed section which also pays homage to the paratroopers who fought on D-Day.

In 1962, the museum was built by the town's mayor, Michel de Vallavieille, in one of the original German bunkers. Michel was mistaken as a German and was gravely wounded by an American soldier during the war, but he never held a grudge and always felt grateful for the sacrifices of the many people who fought on D-Day to free their town. At first, the town was reluctant to build a museum (the townspeople wanted to forget the horrors of the war) and Michel faced a lot of resistance. However, he prevailed and Michel formed many friendships with people who had been on Utah Beach on D-Day, leading to the donation of many of the items contained in the museum's collection. Michel's son, Charles, is now the curator of the museum and shares his father's commitment to preserving the memory of D-Day while expressing gratitude for the GIs who fought to liberate France.

ST. MARIE DU MONT

St. Marie du Mont fountain

A few miles beyond the seawall of Utah Beach is the town center of St. Marie du Mont, the town GIs would have encountered after storming the beaches. The church, in the center of the town, was used by the Germans because the bell tower was a perfect lookout, seeing all the way to the sea. Realizing this, the Germans, round-the-clock, had a soldier on duty to keep a lookout for an invasion, and the museum has the German telemeter found abandoned in the bell tower after D-Day.

The museum's founder, Michel, and son, Charles, are relatives of the several de Vallavieille family members who are memorialized in the center of town on a monument commemorating WWI (WWII details were later added to the monument). This monument is the backdrop for the famous photograph taken of the 101st Airborne's Easy Company who accomplished their objective at Brecourt Manor and linked up with members of the 4th Infantry Division near the church around noon on D-Day.

JAMES S RODWELL

Valley General, Veteran of Two Wars, Is Indifferent to Medals.

MISSION — Combat duty in World Wars I and II have netted Brig. Gen. J. S. Rodwell a whole assembly of colorful decorations about which he cares very little.

An "old army" man who enlisted in 1916 and went up from the ranks in time to fight in France as an officer in World War I, General Rodwell looks upon battle decorations as a minor item in the business of fighting a war—this in spite of the fact that he has been decorated by the British and the French governments in addition to receiving a full quota of American combat emblems.

Promoted Overseas

Promoted to his present rank while overseas, General Rodwell arrived in the Valley last week after having accompanied a unit of his Fourth Division back from France. Mrs. Rodwell, the former Miss Pauline Drummond of Mission and Rio Grande City, has made her home in the latter city while he was overseas. General Rodwell, a native of New York, is a staunch Texan and claims Rio Grande City, where he has business interests, as his home.

Overseas from January, 1944 until late in June when he sailed for home, General Rodwell has served as assistant commander of the Fourth Division, continuing the assignment he has held since 1940 when the division was reactivated.

At one time during the European campaign, the Fourth fought for 199 days without rest. General Rodwell revealed. No sooner had they been ordered to a rest area than the Battle of the Bulge started and they were returned to combat, continuing that time without rest, until March. Their interim period was four days.

General Rodwell went ashore with his division at H-Hour on D-Day and the 199 days that followed took care of the Cherbourg campaign, St. Lo, the breakthrough of July 25, the liberation of Paris in August, the pursuit across France, the Siegfried Line, the battle of Hurtgen Forest and Luxembourg.

Of all the phases of June-to-December fighting, the Cherbourg offensive was the toughest going, General Rodwell reported, saying that the Fourth participated in the Cherbourg fighting right up to the waterfront.

Honored by France

The Republic of France presented General Rodwell the Order of Chevalier of the Legion of Honor for his part in it. They added the Croix de Guerre for the liberation of Paris. General Rodwell wears them along with the five campaign stars on his ETO ribbon, the bronze spearhead for the invasion, the Silver Star with one cluster, the Bronze Star, the Distinguished Service Cross, and the medal for the British Distinguished Service Order.

General Rodwell's introduction to the Valley came in 1923 when he was assigned to Fort Ringgold for a tour of duty which continued until 1927. It was while he was at the Rio Grande City post that he met Miss Drummond of Mission, daughter of Mr. and Mrs. William Drummond, now of Rio Grande City. He was Miss Drummond's escort when she reigned as queen of the second Valley Mid-Winter Fair at Harlingen. In Mission, he and Mrs. Rodwell have been guests of Mrs. Rodwell's sister, Mrs. George Boyle, and Mr. Boyle. He and the latter are partners in the ownership of Hotel Ringgold at Rio Grande City.

Indifferent to Medals newspaper clipping

In 1916, James Rodwell joined the 2nd Plattsburg Training Camp in New York and was sent overseas with the 2nd Cavalry in WWI. He was a Captain in the first war and is credited with being the first officer to lead the cavalry to the front. At the end of WWI, he graduated from Cavalry School, the Infantry School Advanced Course, and the

Command and General Staff School. Between WWI and WWII, he was stationed in various locations including Ft. Ringgold, Texas, Ft. Leavenworth, Kansas, and New York City. As a Colonel, he was assigned to the 4th Infantry Division when it was reactivated in 1940. He was General Barton's Chief of Staff and commander of the 8th Infantry Regiment. He rose to the rank of Brigadier General in WWII, was Assistant Division Commander beginning October of 1944, and participated in all five campaigns of the European Theater. Brigadier General James S. Rodwell was a decorated veteran of both world wars (with medals from WWII that included the Distinguished Service Cross, Silver Star with oak leaf cluster, Legion of Merit with oak leaf cluster, Bronze Star with oak leaf cluster, British Distinguished Service Order, French Croix de Guerre with palm, Legion d'Honneur, and the Combat Infantryman Badge). He retired in 1946, the same year as General Barton and General Blakeley. After retiring from the army, James restored and managed the historic La Borde Hotel which he and his brother-in-law purchased in 1939. He renamed the hotel "Hotel Ringgold" after nearby Fort Ringgold where he was stationed when he met his wife whom he married in 1927. Upon retirement from the hotel business, James and his wife moved to Colorado where they built a home in which to live the remainder of their lives. They did not have any children, but remained close to Robert's widow and children. Brigadier James S. Rodwell died on December 27, 1962 in a Colorado hospital.

ROBERT L. RODWELL

Robert Rodwell and wife, Rose (Grandma Rose was named after her)

Robert Rodwell, Uncle Jim's brother, was born in 1896 in Clyde, New York and died on April 12, 1924 in Syracuse, New York. All details pertaining to Robert, Uncle Jim, Rose, and the family are accurate, including the deaths of Robert's and Jim's parents and Robert's accident. Uncle Jim and Robert were extremely close, and, when Robert died, Uncle Jim made every effort to foster close relationships with Robert's children. Uncle Jim did not have children of his own, and his gift to his niece and nephews was being a link to the father they lost.

THE 4TH INFANTRY DIVISION

On June 6, 1944, the 8th Infantry Regiment of the 4th Infantry Division was the first to land on Utah Beach, spearheading the Normandy invasion. The 4th Infantry Division was the first to enter Paris and the first to enter Germany as well. In WWII, the 4th Infantry Division was in contact with the enemy for 199 consecutive days and then continued to engage the remaining months of the occupation. There were four brief periods of rest throughout their engagement in the European Theater, but other than those periods, the Division fought continuously. No other division saw as much action as the 4th Infantry Division, nor did any other suffer as many casualties. By the end of an eleven-month period, the 4th Infantry Division had fought in all five European campaigns, credited with the successful completion of all assigned objectives.

WWII TIMELINE
4th Infantry Division

JANUARY 26, 1944
4ID arrives in England

JUNE 6, 1944
4ID, led by 8th Infantry Regiment, is first seaborne division to land on D-Day, Utah Beach

This begins 4ID's 336 days of fighting until VE Day on May 8, 1945

JUNE 25, 1944
4ID and 9ID liberate Cherbourg

4ID continues hedgerow fighting through July 1944

JULY 25, 1944
4ID leads St. Lo Breakout, Operation Cobra

4ID continues to engage, pushing through France

AUGUST 25, 1944
Paris is liberated. 4ID's 12th Infantry Regiment first to enter Paris

4ID continues pursuit of retreating German army

SEPTEMBER 11, 1944
4ID's 22nd Infantry Regiment first Allied unit to cross Siegfried Line and enter Germany

Bitter fighting continues in Siegfried Line through September

NOVEMBER 6, 1944
4ID's 12th Infantry Regiment enters Hurtgen Forest, rest of 4ID enters the fight on November 16

4ID remains engaged through December, bloodiest fight of the war for 4ID, four Medals of Honor earned

DECEMBER 16, 1944
Battle of the Bulge begins, 4ID holds southern shoulder in Luxembourg

Patton letter to MG Barton: "Your most recent fight... when you halted the left shoulder of the German thrust into the American lines... is the most outstanding accomplishment of yourself and your division."

FEBRUARY 1945
Often occupying the same foxholes they dug in Sept., 4ID again penetrates Siegfried Line

4ID fights through Prum and other German strongholds

MARCH - APRIL 1945
4ID pursues Germans across their homeland

MAY 8, 1945
Victory in Europe, VE Day

4ID is relieved and placed on occupational duty

When Germany surrendered on May 8, 1945, the 4th Infantry Division had participated in all five European campaigns, from D-Day to VE Day, fighting almost continuously for 11 months, with over 30,000 casualties

ACKNOWLEDGEMENTS

A very special thank you to my husband and family for your patience. I know that I become completely obsessed and driven, and I know that it was not always easy to lose me to my work or to participate in endless conversations about my research. Without your support, I could not have shared the legacy that has become very important to me. I love you.

Thank you to Charles and Véronique de Vallavieille for opening your home, your museum, your family's history, your town's doors, and your hearts to me. You made my visit to France a once-in-a-lifetime experience filled with awe, tears, and a deep sense of purpose. Your kindness and generosity are significant to the cane's journey and your friendship has made my heart full. I cannot express how truly extraordinary my visit was because of you.

Thanks are also due to Séverine Diaz, Benoit Noel, Flavie Poisson, and Véronique Baugin who made the cane's journey to France possible and the experience extraordinary. To Séverine and Véronique for sharing in the travel adventure and the many hours of driving. Additionally, to Séverine, beyond the traveling, thanks also for the coordination of the visit, and for your friendship which is appreciated more than you can know. To Benoit for being my first connection in France and for sharing the excitement of the cane's discovery, for being part of the adventure in Meautis as a fellow detective, and for expertly packing my "sand baby" for safe travels back to the states. To Flavie for guiding the Normandy adventure, translating, teaching, sharing your knowledge with me, and embracing me in friendship; I am forever grateful for your many gifts that continue beyond my visit to France.

Without the help of Bob Babcock, 4ID historian and owner of Deeds Publishing—providing after action reports, giving detailed factual information, checking my narrative for historical accuracy, publishing my "baby," and sharing a love for the 4th Infantry Division—this book would have been subpar at best. Additionally, for your enthusiasm and support for this project, I am forever grateful. Connecting with you was absolutely "meant to be."

Thank you to my friends who supported and encouraged me from Day 1: from sharing excitement over the discoveries to pushing me to write this book, I wouldn't be here without you. Thank you all for your continued friendship and love. I am afraid that if I list the names, someone will be left off the list as an error of my brain, not my heart! So, you know who you are (my literacy buddies, my summer Monday friends, my forever friends, my educational partners, Patrica cugini and cugine, etc.)…I appreciate you!

A special thanks to Christopher A. Stewart and Evan Kenneth DuFresne for the gift of Uncle Jim's words. Stumbling upon an obscure online citation led to a shared document that I truly treasure. Thank you for the work you do to preserve soldiers' legacies.

Thanks to Anthony Lewis and Alan Roptin for making the experience at the Normandy American Cemetery private, meaningful, and special. It is very hard to describe that day to anyone who was not present and I feel honored to have shared those moments with you. It is a day that will live in my heart forever.

My gratitude to Stephen Bourque for sharing your research gems with me. The personal letters and the war time diary you shared with me have become treasures.

To my brother for acquiescing. I know it has not been easy to have a bossy, older sister, even as an adult. I appreciate you allowing this journey to happen (even though you wanted to keep the cane), and I promise to pay you back in shipments of Pommeau de Normandie.

Thank you to my dad for sharing your vast knowledge of WWII and military history, for being part of the cane's discovery, and for being patient with my never-ending quest for more boxes. You have been beyond generous with your time and with your love. Although I know my endless hunting for details has been exhausting at times, it has all been more meaningful with you as an integral part. I am very lucky to have you as my father and my friend.

Final thanks to my mom, without whom none of this would be possible. Not only are you my biological connection to Uncle Jim, but you are my biggest cheerleader, favorite editor, and trusted friend. You shared the excitement as we unpacked boxes and cried with me as items were discovered. You have been the first person with whom I needed to share every detail of each experience as this adventure unfolded and you supported the journey every step of the way. Thank you.

ABOUT THE AUTHOR

Writer, teacher, genealogist, wellness enthusiast, and history junkie, Elizabeth Rieman lives in Ohio with her husband, son, and dog, Stella. When not working or spending time with family, she can frequently be found presenting to various groups, showing others that every story matters and that family histories deserve to be preserved. Her latest release, *Unpacking Yesterday: Brotherhood's Legacy*, fulfills her personal mission to make permanent the legacies of those whose lives have shaped us and have made us who we are.

You can write to her online at bethrieman11@gmail.com.

CPSIA information can be obtained
at www.ICGtesting.com
Printed in the USA
FSHW010051210720
72329FS